MW00935163

Out of Darkness

Book #2 of the Heaven Hill Series

By Laramie Briscoe

Copyright

Edited by: Lindsay Gray Hopper
https://www.facebook.com/EditingbyLindsay

Proofread by: Sherri Gardner
http://www.writewordsproof.com

Cover Design by: Kari Ayasha of Cover to Cover Designs
covertocoverdesigns.com

Photography by: Kelsey Keeton/©2013 K Keeton Designs
kkeetondesigns.com

Cover Models: Coltyn Seifert & Jaclyn Rutland

Motorcycle courtesy of: Nathan Currys Hotrods Custom Paint
https://www.facebook.com/nathan.curry.10

Dedication

This is for anyone who's coming out of a bad place in their lives. No matter how dark the moment seems — there will always be a way out of it.

To my family, friends, co-workers, and fans...thank you from the bottom of my heart!

Summary

Ex-news reporter.
Rape survivor.
Former enemy of the Heaven Hill MC.

Meredith Rager's life completely changed the night she was attacked by an unknown person. Once a vibrant force that threatened everything about Heaven Hill, she is now under their care. The only place she feels safe is inside their compound. When she decides to take back the part of her life that her rapist took away, she discovers secrets that once again could tear the club apart.

Orphan.
Formidable force of nature.
Loved member of the Heaven Hill MC.

Tyler Blackfoot came into the world a John Doe. An orphan from the moment that he took his first breath, the only thing anyone knew was his Native American heritage. For most of his life, he's been alone – except for the club that has taken him in as their own. When he rescued Meredith, a protective side of his personality came out that he never knew he had. Protecting her means everything – even when he discovers danger might be closer than either of them thought possible.

Together, the two of them are trying to make a life for themselves. Against everything they have, they're hoping to see the light that will lead them out of darkness.

Chapter One

For services rendered.

Meredith jerked awake as she remembered the dollar bill hitting her back. It was the same dream every night. She always woke up when he said those words and threw the money. Sleep never came after one of her nightmares, even when she took the pills the good doc had prescribed. Carefully, she pushed back the covers of Tyler's bed and slid her legs to the side. Her heart caught, the way it always did when she saw Tyler asleep on the floor. Maybe one day she would be able to invite him into this bed. Quietly, she dressed and grabbed her running shoes. If she couldn't sleep, she may as well get something accomplished.

Making her way to the kitchen of the clubhouse, she smiled and waved at those who had come to know her in the weeks she'd been staying here. It was easy to pretend with these people that nothing really had happened to her. She'd taken a leave of absence from her job and moved all her belongings into storage. Meredith had known without a doubt that she could never go back to the life that she had lived before. Any of it. Now her time was broken into two points – before the rape and after the rape.

"Going for a run?" Liam asked as he spotted her running shoes.

"Yeah, is Denise up yet?"

The look that overtook his face when she mentioned his woman made Meredith sad. At one time that was what she wanted, and she wasn't sure she'd ever get back there again.

"Sure is, she was on her way up here. Just text her. I know she'd love to run with you."

It went without saying that Meredith didn't like to run by herself, and Denise usually went along whether she wanted to or not. Meredith was beginning to understand that it was a sign of a real friendship.

"Will you let Tyler know where I am?" she asked, grabbing a couple bottles of water.

"I will, but you and I both know that he *always* knows where you are."

Not long after her attack, Tyler had installed a special tracking program on her phone. Before, it would have freaked her out. Now though, it made her feel safe.

"See ya," she called to the VP as she made her way out the back door.

Stepping out into the sunlight, she looked up. It was coming upon mid-October in south central Kentucky and it should have been at least a little bit chilly, but they were in the grips of an Indian summer. For reasons she couldn't understand, Meredith was glad. She wasn't sure she could face a winter being cooped up right now. Being outside in this protected place was the only way she felt safe. The only time she felt alive other than when she wrote.

Writing had become her solace. She wrote something every day. The therapist had suggested it, and she had been amazed at how much she enjoyed it. Although she'd been a reporter, she'd never really been a writer. She loved it even more than the news.

"You ready, girlfriend?"

Meredith smiled, the first genuine one she'd had all day, as she spotted Denise walking towards her, pulling her hair into a ponytail.

"I don't know why you do that. You always end up taking it down because it gives you a headache."

Denise grinned. "Makes me feel like I'm a real athlete."

A laugh bubbled up from deep within Meredith, and she put her hand over her mouth to cover it up.

"Don't," Denise admonished. "It's good to hear you laugh."

It went without saying between the two of them that Meredith hadn't had much to laugh about for a while.

"It feels good *to* laugh," she admitted softly.

The moment got a little heavy, and Denise did what she'd gotten best at with the other woman, turned the attention away from her.

"So how far are we going to go today? Are you going to give me a heart attack or just an irregular heartbeat?" she joked.

Meredith knew just how much Denise hated exercise, and that said a lot about the person that Denise was. That she came out here everyday, huffing and puffing her way through whatever run Meredith mapped out for them.

"Maybe just an irregular heartbeat. I don't wanna kill ya just yet."

"Thank God for small favors."

With that, the two took off, jogging slowly, but Denise groaned because she knew that soon they would really start running, and that just plain sucked.

"Meredith go for a run?"

It unnerved Liam how quiet Tyler was when he wanted to be. Sometimes he could come in and out of a room and no one knew it, even if the room was full of people.

"Yeah, you could just track her, you know."

"I know," he said, grabbing the handle of his skull coffee cup. "But then I feel like I'm stalking her. It's not a good feeling."

"She still having trouble sleeping?" Liam asked his friend as he took a seat across the table from him.

"Yeah, she thinks I don't know, but I hear her every morning when she wakes up. She's having nightmares, but she won't talk to anybody about them. I keep hoping she'll talk to Denise."

Gently, Liam reminded the other man. "She had a horrible thing happen to her. Maybe she doesn't want to talk to *anyone* about it."

"I want her to talk to me about it. That way I can figure out who the fucker was and then scalp him like my ancestors would have."

"You know how scary you are saying that as you drink from a skull coffee mug?" Liam deadpanned.

Tyler grinned. "I know. Keeps you on your toes don't it?"

Denise gulped water from the bottle that Meredith had given her. "You love this don't you?" she panted, putting her hand at the stitch on her side.

"Not at all. It's sad that you're having such a hard time with a simple run," Meredith taunted as she grinned.

"Simple my ass, Rager. These are fucking hills. Hills, I say!"

"I know, and you're doing a really good job. I really am proud of you."

Denise took a moment to get her breath. "I'm proud of you too."

The moment turned awkward, and Meredith turned so that Denise couldn't see her face. "Don't turn away from me. I am proud of you. You've found something that you like doing and you're doing it."

"Only because I know I'm safe here," Meredith argued.

"I worried about you that week after it happened. I didn't think you were ever going to get out of that room. You've made great strides."

"But I still can't let Tyler sleep in his own bed."

Denise cautiously put her hand on Meredith's arm. "Trust me, when you're ready, he'll be ready. No one even looks at you wrong for fear of him."

"I feel like I'm using him," she admitted.

"You're not. You're living your life the only way you know how at this point, and truthfully that's all you can ask for. I can't imagine going through what you went through, and I'm not saying that out of pity. It's the truth."

But that was the problem wasn't it? All Meredith could feel, when she could actually feel, was the pity. The fear. The emptiness. When would it ever change?

Chapter Two

I *wonder what I did to deserve this? Was it really my fault, playing two clubs against one another, searching for the truth? Did I really deserve to be raped? I think I did, and that's probably the worst thing. I try to make myself feel better, I really do, but then I realize that maybe I did ask for this.*

"What are you writing?"

Meredith slammed the leather journal closed and glanced up at Tyler. The man was beautiful really. He stood easily 6'3, though with his motorcycle boots he probably topped 6'5. The Native American heritage was apparent in his high cheekbones, the long, straight black hair, and the suntanned tone of his skin. His brown eyes burned intensely as he watched her.

"Just journaling like the therapist suggested I do."

"Speaking of, are you ready for your appointment?"

She nodded. "I am, just gotta grab my backpack."

Silent as ever, all he did was nod. He was so good to her, taking her wherever she needed to go, never asking for more than what she was willing to give, talking to her only when she spoke to him. It was everything she needed, and she counted on him more than she'd ever thought she would count on another human being. Grabbing her backpack, she put it on and went to stand beside him.

"Ready when you are."

He ushered her out of the room, past the people gathered in the clubhouse, and out to where he parked his bike. Once there, he got on and handed her the helmet that he'd bought for her and waited for her to hop on the bike.

This was his favorite part of the day, when she would put her arms tightly around his waist and hang on for dear life. It was the only time she allowed him to touch her. Sometimes at night, he would watch her sleep. Very rarely, he would carefully perch himself on the edge of the bed and lightly run his fingertips over her cheek. Everybody thought he was a saint for trying to help her through this time in her life, but he truly was a bastard because of the thoughts he had about her when she would subconsciously nuzzle closer.

Meredith loved the feel of the wind against her face as they rode the bike along the back roads of Warren County. Luckily for her, the therapist that had been recommended was more of a country doctor, catering to most of the uninsured in the community. She didn't even have to go into the city for her appointments. Tyler revved the bike as they went around a curve, and she risked a smile. She knew it was for her. She loved the little jump it gave, and it always made her squeal and tighten her arms around his flat midsection.

They got to the old farmhouse the doctor used for an office, and Tyler turned off the bike, balancing it with his long legs so she could get off.

"You want me to stick around or take off?"

She wasn't sure how long this session would last. She had some things she wanted to discuss, and she didn't want to be rushed.

"You can take off if you want, I don't know how long this'll take."

"You're okay, right?" he asked, concern marring his face.

"I am, but I need to talk some things through. I don't want you to have to wait on me."

"You know it's not a problem for me to do that, right?"

She gave him a small smile. "I know, Tyler, but you go do something for yourself okay. I'm giving you a break from babysitter duty."

"Don't do that. I'm not 'babysitting' you. I wouldn't be here if I didn't want to be." It bothered him that she just assumed she knew his mind, knew what he wanted to do. His temper spiked, but he kept it under control for her.

Meredith could tell what it cost him not to talk back to her, not to raise his voice and show anger. It simmered there below the surface and she could see it, but he wouldn't unleash on her. A part of her wished he would. Another part worried what would happen when he exploded one day. Instead, she sighed, talking calmly.

"I know, and I can't tell you how much I appreciate it."

He gave her a salute as he started the bike and roared off. Squaring her shoulders, Meredith took a deep breath and entered the house.

"How has your week been going, Meredith?"

Doctor Jones was an older woman. She had salt and pepper gray hair and the demeanor of a grandmother. Meredith loved talking with her.

"It's been going. I'm still having trouble sleeping. I can get to sleep a lot easier now, but it's the staying asleep I'm having trouble with."

"Is Tyler still sleeping in the room with you?"

Meredith blushed. "He is, but still on the floor."

"Has he made any kind of move to try and get back in his bed or move you out?"

"Not at all. I guess that's what unnerves me."

Doctor Jones sat forward. "Unnerves you how?"

"What if he wants to get back into his bed, but what if he doesn't want me to be there?"

Her brows knitted in confusion. "I'm not sure I'm following."

"What if he has male urges, but he knows that I'm not going to satisfy them."

"Oh, you're wondering if he wants to bring a woman home for sex?"

Meredith nodded, her face going red.

"Now, are you blushing, or are you jealous?" Meredith ran her sweaty palms along her jean clad thighs.

She watched as the doctor made notes in her notebook. It felt like this answer held a lot of weight. Like if she got it wrong, she would never be the woman she had been before.

"A little bit of both. Is that bad?"

"Not at all, Meredith. You've had a tragedy, but you aren't dead. I've seen the man. You'd have to *be* dead in order not to notice how nice looking he is."

"But what if I'm holding him back? I mean, it's been a month, almost a month and a half, since it happened. I still can't even stand to have a man inadvertently touch me. How long is he going to stand for that?"

The doctor pursed her lips. "Let's break this down Meredith. Has he approached you in any way?"

"Well no, but that doesn't mean that I haven't thought about it. I just don't think I can act on it again – ever."

"Why don't you do this? Why don't you explain to him your feelings and see if you can start out small. The two of you are friends, right? Maybe you should concentrate on spending time one-on-one. Get used to him that way and then see if he'll take you out on a date. I warn you, if you move too swiftly you could set yourself back."

Meredith knew in her heart that was true. She also knew that she was the only person here trying to rush herself. For some reason, she didn't doubt Tyler would wait for her forever. It just made her nervous, the number of women who hung around the clubhouse. They all had their eyes on either Tyler or Liam, and now with Liam spoken for they, were almost all exclusively coming for Tyler. She wanted to stake her claim, but she didn't know how.

"I'll do that. I'll talk to him about maybe spending some one-on-one time together. Ya know, outside of the bedroom." Nervously she nodded, wetting her dry lips with her tongue.

"You set the pace for this, Meredith. As long as you feel comfortable, it can go at whatever pace you want it to. There is no right or wrong. Remember that."

Chapter Three

Her watch showed he was late. Tyler was never late, especially to pick her up from her appointment. Tucking her lip in between her teeth, she contemplated if she should call him. Would that be too similar to her acting like a girlfriend? Putting her thumb over his number in her contacts, she was about to press dial when she heard the roar of his bike.

As he came to a stop in front of her and turned the engine off, he was apologizing. "Sorry I'm late. I was boxing with Layne, and I didn't realize what time it was."

"Boxing?" she asked as she came down the steps of the front porch. Now that she was closer, she could see that his hair was wet. It looked like he had taken a quick shower before he came to get her.

"Yeah. Kinda like you going for a run. Layne and I box. He has the same kind of temper as me."

Layne, she knew, was a Prospect who had been over in Iraq as a member of the armed forces. He probably did have a lot of aggression to get rid of. "I understand, I was just worried."

"It's the only way I can keep from showing you my anger," he admitted. "I don't want to scare you, but sometimes I want so badly to find the fucker and beat his brains out that I've just got to release it somehow."

She understood exactly where he was coming from. When she was ready, she wanted to find him and do the exact same thing. "I know," she told him softly as she got on the back of the bike.

He breathed a sigh of relief when she didn't hold herself away from him. Business as usual. It was just him that felt disoriented on this day.

She couldn't breathe. Her face was being held down in the dirt, and dusty soil coated her tongue, making it heavy. Meredith tried with everything she had to scream, but all she kept getting were mouthfuls of earth. All of a sudden she started to choke. It caused her to panic, and she began to hyperventilate, trying to breathe air into her lungs. Clawing with her nails, she fought against the weight pressing her down, but she could not get it off her. Her back ached as she tried to throw the heaviness off. Thrashing her head back and forth, she fought to get either air in or dirt out. It didn't matter which.

"Meredith."

A deep voice, one she knew, called her name. She wanted to go to that voice. It represented safety and warmth. When she heard it, she didn't feel cold. Struggling to lift her eyes open, she continued to fight.

"Meredith, open those eyes. Stop fighting me. You're gonna hurt yourself. C'mon honey, open them eyes."

It was the endearment that got her. He never used them, and it put a warm spot in her torso where her heart beat wildly. She wanted to see him say these words to her. With a start, she awoke.

Opening her eyes, she took stock of what was going on. Her nails dug into Tyler's biceps, holding him away from her. She had been kicking her feet and his arm lay over them to prevent her from kicking him.

"Oh no, are you okay?"

"I'm fine. Are *you* okay?" The tenderness in his eyes was almost her undoing.

"You need to talk to the doctor about not being able to sleep without having these nightmares." It killed him to hear her call out in her sleep, to watch her fight the unknown assailant. It pissed him off; made him want to find the man and rip his heart out.

"She told me once that when I'm ready to get over it, my nightmares will go away. I'm still hanging on to something, I guess." What that something was, she didn't know, but obviously it had a tight grip on her.

He wanted to know what it was. What had such a hold on her that she couldn't sleep at night?

"When I find him and kill him, you'll sleep perfectly."

Her heart hated when he said things like that, but her mind agreed with him. She wanted him to find the man that had hurt her and punish him. Meredith wanted him dead.

Chapter Four

I went to the grocery store yesterday, and I was scared to death. Some kid dressed up for Halloween and looked just like my attacker. I had a complete meltdown in the middle of the store. What does that say about me? Even I can tell I've been shaken ever since. I don't think I've been this fragile since the actual attack. Last night I barely slept at all. I even heard Tyler come to bed. I've never heard him come in the room before. I'm so on edge, I don't know what to do. I feel like I need to reclaim some piece of myself, but I'm not sure how to do that. I want to feel like I can protect myself and hold it together. I need some kinda outlet besides writing because I feel rage beginning to overtake my personality. I'm starting to get angry and I don't want to take that out on Tyler. He admitted to me that he's been boxing with Layne. That they beat the shit out of each other and that's the only way he can come to me without the anger. I'm not sure that it's healthy, but it's got to be better than what I'm doing. Which is absolutely nothing. How can I take back yet another part of myself that I didn't even know I'd lost?

Breakfast was well underway when Meredith finally made it to the kitchen. Tyler sat at one side of the table drinking from his skull mug. She couldn't help but notice that everyone gave him a wide berth at breakfast. It was wide most of the time, but breakfast was a different kind of wide.

"Is this seat taken?" she asked as she walked over to where he sat.

"I think you know it's being saved for you."

She couldn't help but smile a little. He didn't flirt often, but when he did, it was very cute. "Are people scared of you?" she asked, indicating his mug.

Leaning as close as he dared, he whispered. "Word has it that it's sacred. Not many people want to touch it, and nobody else wants to drink out of it. They're afraid of what might happen."

Her eyes narrowed. "Are you tellin' the truth or are you pullin' my leg?"

"You wanna take a drink and find out?" he asked, an innocent look on his face.

That seemed so intimate, drinking after him. Before her attack, she would never have given it a second thought. Now though, it felt like something that couples would do. "No, that's okay."

She watched as he brought the mug back up to his lips and took another drink of the hot coffee. The skin underneath his eyes was dark, and she could see that he was tired. Had her nightmares been keeping him up more than she realized?

"Somethin' you wanna ask me?"

Her fingers twisted, and he could see her hem and haw. "Just spit it out."

"If someone wanted to know how to defend themselves — not like self-defense classes where you have to touch each other, but some other kind of defense — what would you tell them to do?"

This was for her. He wasn't stupid. His only hope was that she was finally getting to the anger side of her grief because until she got angry, she would never be able to overcome it, and he would never be able to get revenge.

"I'd tell you that you need to learn to shoot. Want me to take you?"

He'd given her a gun for protection once before, but she didn't know how to use it. If push came to shove, she figured she could just point, shoot, and pray for the best. Now though, in this stage of her recovery, she wanted the instruction. She wanted to know how to defend herself if she ever had to. It would be unfair to count on Tyler forever.

"Would you?"

"If you want to learn, I'd be happy to teach you. You wanna go today?" His dark eyes took in the vibrant light that lit up her face. Finally something was coming through besides the darkness. Would she accept it or would this just be something else she talked herself out of?

"Can we?" It felt like she was putting him on the spot. "If you have other plans, you realize you can say no."

"I don't have any other plans." And even if he did, he would never say a word to her because this was something she wanted and needed. He would disappoint a million other people before he said no to her.

She nodded. "I don't want to monopolize your time if you have something else to do."

"Trust me, nobody else matters as much as you do right now," he admitted softly.

Meredith didn't know what to do with that knowledge. It scared her and made her happy, all at the same time. While it excited her that he said those kinds of words to her, it also caused her to wonder what he was giving up for her. What was he not telling her?

"Don't look at me like that," he frowned. "Like I've told you before, if I didn't want to be here, I wouldn't be. Just because you're having doubts – don't throw that on me."

With those words he had read her mind. She could tell it pissed him off by the way his eyes narrowed, but he kept it in check for her. Tyler was so nice to her, but she just kept throwing it back in his face. When would she be able to just accept the nice things he wanted to do for her and live a normal life?

"It's very heavy," she told him as she stood with a gun in her hand.

"It's supposed to be. It means business, and you mean business by holding it. Nobody's gonna mistake you for a pushover with you pointing that at their chest."

He had taught her gun safety and how to stand. "Now, I want you to line it up and shoot it. Watch for the kick-back," he cautioned.

Doing everything he'd taught her, she cursed as it kicked back on her, making her shot go wide.

"Brace with your hand on the butt of it," he instructed.

She did as he instructed and shot again, but again it went wide when it kicked back.

"What am I doing wrong?" Meredith was getting irritated. In her old life she had been good at everything. It had been required by her parents for her to be good at everything. If they could see her now, they would probably be looking down their noses. To her knowledge, no one in her family had ever owned a gun or hung out with a motorcycle gang. Leave it to her to break the mold.

His long legs ate up the distance between them. "I'm going to stand behind you and put my arms around you. Okay?"

Not sure how she felt about the situation, she nodded anyway. When he cozied up to her back, she inhaled deeply, smelling his masculine scent as well as the leather of his cut. Carefully, he put his arms around her and put his hands over top of hers. He was so much bigger than her, but she never felt threatened by him. His chest was hard against her back, and she wanted to snuggle up to it. Shockingly, her nipples hardened when he moved his arms back, inadvertently brushing the underside of her breast. His deep voice lulled her, and she just tried to enjoy the feelings for a few moments.

The chest behind her was hard, a solid wall of muscle that told her just how strong he was. Closing her eyes against the panic, she thought back to that night, how that man had boxed her in and she hadn't been able to get up. Her mind told her that this was Tyler, not her rapist, but that didn't stop the quickening of her heart. *Stop it, Meredith! He's the one person who's not going to hurt you. Just allow this to happen,* she told herself.

"Are you even listening to me?" his voice held a tone of frustration.

"Sorry, what were you saying?"

"That it's important to pay attention when you're aiming your gun."

His double meaning wasn't lost on her, and her cheeks heated. She shook her head to clear her thoughts and concentrated on paying attention while he told her what to do.

"You ready to do this on your own?" he asked.

"I think so."

Tyler didn't want to let her go. Every time she came to him willingly, it was that much harder to release her. He hated the hold that monster had on her. Hated that he couldn't seem to break through the walls she had erected around herself. He understood them, but hated them just the same. Reluctantly, he stepped back from her. He set up some targets for her, and then watched as she aimed and fired, knocking every one of them down.

"That's what I'm talking about!" He raced over, giving her a high five.

Excitement caused her to launch herself into his arms. She hugged him tightly before realization smacked her in the face. His face wore an expression of shock before he disentangled himself from her.

Brushing her confusion off, she cleared her throat. "I can't believe I just did that," she smiled.

The feeling was exhilarating as she realized that she had made a move to protect herself. With his encouragement she had learned to do something she'd never thought she would be able to do.

"You *did* do it. I'm so proud of you."

She beamed for the first time in a long time. Pleasure shone on her face, and he basked in the glory of it. The words she spoke next made up for everything he'd been through with her. "Ya know what? I'm proud of me too."

Chapter Five

"Meredith, it's been a week since our last session. How have things been going?"

She looked at the doctor, avoiding her eyes. This was supposed to be helping her, but it would never help her if she didn't come clean. That was something she realized now more than ever. Especially after the events of the last seven days. She took a deep breath and began talking to Doctor Jones.

"I've had an interesting week. I finally went out and about with someone besides Tyler and it was a complete disaster."

"Why was that?"

"Denise took me to the grocery. Well, the grocery also has Halloween costumes for sale. I nearly had a panic attack because of the number of people in the store. Then at the checkout, some guy bumped into me. I looked behind me, and he was dressed exactly like my attacker was. He was so excited that his Halloween costume scared me, and I took off running. It brought back everything and I damn near passed out in the parking lot. I also had another nightmare that night."

Doctor Jones took in the paleness of her face and the dark circles under her eyes. "Do you have nightmares a lot? That's something you've never really been open about. You've mentioned it once, and I told you that you weren't ready to get over whatever was bothering you, but if you're having them every night there may be an issue."

"I have them every night. Tyler wakes me up and tries to calm me down. Sometimes it works, sometimes it doesn't."

"What happens in your nightmares?"

The room began to close in on Meredith, but she knew that she had to get this out. The collar of her shirt felt tight, and she reached up to pull it away from her neck. "I re-live the attack. Sometimes it's just parts of it. Sometimes it's the whole thing. There's one thing that gets me every time. He threw a dollar bill on me afterwards. He said it was for 'services rendered'. That's usually where it ends."

Doctor Jones' face paled. In her experience, something that crass – it was personal and it caused fear to clench her stomach for her patient.

"How do you feel when Tyler wakes you up and it's over?"

She hated when Doctor Jones asked her redundant questions like this, but knew she was just trying to get to the bottom of her feelings. "I used to feel so sad, like I could completely breakdown and just curl in a ball and die. Now I feel angry. There's a part of me that wants to find this guy and throw a dollar bill on him. Then there's the part of me that's scared shitless of doing it."

"Anger is good, that means you've moving on in the grief stage."

"That's what Tyler said," she chuckled. "I guess I should also report that I asked Tyler to teach me how to shoot a gun."

"How did he react to that?" Doctor Jones smiled.

"He took me out to the shooting range and taught me gun safety and how to shoot. I did it and actually hit the target after a little practice. That's the first time I've been proud of myself in a long time. I should also mention, I had a reaction to Tyler." She said the last part softly.

"Okay, first of all, let me say I'm proud of you. You decided you were ready to take your safety into your own hands and you did something about it. I would caution you to not go all vigilante, be sure and keep your anger under control. Save it for the shooting range."

Meredith completely understood where the older woman was coming from and greatly appreciated the warning. "I understand," she nodded.

"Now, about your reaction to Tyler. Define reaction."

This made her very uncomfortable. Even before she had been attacked, her sexuality wasn't blatant. She was the type of person to read erotic romances on her e-reader, but balk when a boyfriend asked if he could smack her ass. She wanted it, but didn't want to admit that she wanted it. It was always hard for her to tell someone what she wanted, even if that meant a lot of her desires were unfulfilled because she wasn't vocal about it. Her parents hadn't been the type to kiss or make sexual advances towards each other in front of her. It wasn't until she'd moved out and gone to college that she'd noticed those things between couples. She crossed her legs and put her hands between her knees.

"This makes me very uncomfortable," she openly admitted.

"It's alright, it's just us here. You know that whatever you say doesn't go out these doors."

"I know, but it's hard for me to put into words what I'm feeling."

Doctor Jones sat forward so that the two of them were eye to eye. "I'm not blowing smoke up your ass here, but let me be real honest with you. You've done a complete 180 since you started coming to these sessions. Do you remember the first one? You barely said five words to me. We've been patient with each other and now look at how much you're opening up. It's the same with anything in your life. You have to be patient. It will all come to you if you keep working on it. I have no doubt that you will achieve everything you want to, and I look forward to seeing it. If it takes you two hours to get through this, it's fine. I've got time."

That's what she needed to hear. Feeling more empowered than she had in weeks, she took a deep breath and began. "I'm attracted to Tyler. I was way before that night, we had a flirtation with each other. It wasn't anything huge, but it was obvious we liked each other. It seemed like fate that he found me the night of the attack. From the first moment I met him, I felt safe around him, even though he scared me with how large of a man he is."

That was news to Dr. Jones. "He found you the night of the rape?"

"Yes," she nodded. "He is the one who made me see a doctor, and he stayed with me until it was all over. That was the night he took me back to the clubhouse and began sleeping on the floor. He's been doing it ever since." A thought hit her out of nowhere, causing her to worry. "You don't think I have misguided feelings for him because he is my knight in shining armour do you?"

It was obvious that the doctor thought this question over before she answered. "If you had just met him the night of the attack, then I would say yes. The fact remains that the two of you knew each other before this, and you admitted that you already had an attraction to him. I don't think you have a hero complex."

Meredith sighed with relief. "So we've been closer since I started staying at the clubhouse. I can't bring myself to go home because I'm so scared that whoever did this to me will come back again. I let my lease go and put most of my stuff in storage. I'm pretty much living with him. There have been a few times when I've looked at him as a woman, but I've never been aroused. I can't let myself go there."

"But that changed recently?" The doc guessed.

"It did," she nodded, bringing her arms up around her waist. "He took me out shooting, and I wasn't getting my stance or hold of the gun completely right. He was so thoughtful, he asked before he came up behind me and then showed me how to do it with his own hands."

"How did that make you feel?"

"At first I flinched, and I know he felt it because he got tense. His coming up behind me brought back some memories. But when his hands went around mine and his hard chest pressed against my back, all I could think of was him." She closed her eyes and transported to that one moment in time. "He smelled so good, so masculine. The scent of his leather cut and the scent that is just him surrounded me, and it was like coming home. Then out of nowhere, I got turned on. I'm not sure whether he noticed or not, but my nipples got hard," she whispered, embarrassed to be sharing this with someone else.

The older woman laughed. "That's good, Meredith. It's not a bad thing at all."

"It was mortifying! I won't let the man sleep in his own bed, but I could have *climbed him like a tree* right at that moment," laughter bubbled up in her throat, and in that instant she let go of all the tension that she'd held in her body. She doubled over, tears coming to her eyes as she giggled.

Doctor Jones joined her, so happy that she was having this breakthrough. "That's a perfect description of Tyler, I think. He's a tall man," she acknowledged.

"That he is. I was so happy I had that reaction, but at the same time it made me *so* uncomfortable. It's like my mind and body are constantly at war with one another. One part wants to move on, while the other part won't let me. I know he is a major part of that. I wouldn't be where I am today if it wasn't for him. These mixed signals are going to piss him off sooner or later."

"That's fine and expected. Like I said, with patience you will get to where you need to be. You've already made tremendous strides already. You are moving right along in your progress, and I'm very happy about that."

After the session, Meredith sat on the front porch of the doctor's office, waiting for Tyler to come and get her. For the first time in a long time, it felt like she was breathing again. She could see the blue color of the sky, smell the coming of winter, and feel the breeze against her skin. As she heard the roar of a motorcycle, goose bumps popped up on her arms in anticipation of seeing Tyler again. When he rounded the curve of the driveway and came into sight, Meredith smiled and waved at him. Caught off guard, he waved back. Coming to a stop, he turned the motorcycle off and balanced it, waiting for her to hop on.

"Good session?" he inquired, handing over her helmet.

"Very good session."

The heart stopping smile he gave her was her reward for the basket of emotions she'd felt while spilling her guts. She put her arms around him, holding tightly around his waist, and put her cheek up to the leather on his back.

She had never done this before, and it again caught Tyler off guard. Tentatively, he placed his gloved hand over hers where it was clasped around his waist and gave a squeeze. When she didn't pull back, he smiled to himself. Her trust felt better than anything else ever had in his life and gave him hope as to their future. Giving it another squeeze, he let go and started the bike. Because he knew she liked it, he revved the engine and gunned it so that it took off with a jump. The sound of her laughter made it to his ears, and he grinned as they made their way down the road and back to the clubhouse. He wasn't sure what had happened, but he was happy for it. Happier than he'd been in a very long time.

Chapter Six

"Oh my God, this is the grossest thing ever," Meredith squealed, causing Tyler and Liam to laugh.

The group of them were in Liam's kitchen, preparing to honor a time-tested tradition.

"I'd have to agree, and I've had children," Denise squealed along with her, causing the guys to double over with laughter.

"You think it's so funny, you two do it."

Tyler sighed, taking pity on Meredith, and stood up from the kitchen table. He took off his cut and his shirt, obviously not wanting it to get dirty. Meredith's mouth went dry as the Sahara as he walked over. Funny as it sounded, she'd never seen him without a shirt on before. He was very careful with his nakedness when it came to her. She gawked appreciatively. It was obvious he worked out, the man had what looked like an eight pack on his stomach, and his arm muscles bulged as well, veins showing in his forearms. While she had seen the tattoos on his forearms, she'd never seen the full sleeves or the ones that marked his back and chest. One in particular made her

28

breath catch. It was an amazingly real looking dream catcher that obviously represented his Native American heritage.

"You want my help or not?" he asked, quirking an eyebrow. The slight smile on his face showed his amusement at her perusal of his body.

"Be my guest." She stepped back, going over to the kitchen sink and washing her hands. "Carving pumpkins seemed like such a good idea."

"Agreed," Denise muttered, pulling her hand out of the middle of the pumpkin she'd cut the top off of. The slimy insides clung to her hand as she made a face and slung it onto a plastic bag they'd put on the counter. "But geez, this is so gross," she shivered.

"Here, let me help you, baby." Liam finally got up, amusement on his face.

"'Bout time."

The two women had a seat at the kitchen table and watched as the men cleaned the guts of the pumpkins out. Tyler grinned as he scraped the side of it with the tool from the pumpkin carving kit.

"I've always wanted to do this, and it's as nasty as I had hoped."

His grin reminded Meredith of a little kid, opening a Christmas gift for the first time.

"You've never carved a pumpkin before?" she couldn't keep the surprise out of her voice.

"Never. It wasn't really something that orphanages or foster parents took the time out to do," he shrugged.

When he talked about things like that, her heart hurt. She could just imagine him as a small child, trying to have a normal childhood and being punished at every turn.

"Well, thanks to me, you're getting to experience it. My dad always gutted the pumpkin for me, and now I can see why."

He chuckled, grabbing another handful out and flinging it in Liam's direction.

"Dude, that was uncalled for." Liam dodged it, moving his hand out of the way as it splattered the side of his pumpkin. Even though he complained, Liam loved this. It was the show of camaraderie and family that he wanted to bring so badly to the forefront of their club. William, President of their club and father to Liam and Roni, would have bitched that they were being silly, but these were the moments he knew they all lived for when they did such dangerous things.

"Cut the shit. If you woulda thought about it first, you would have already put it in my hair."

"Yeah, you're probably right," Liam laughed.

"So what are we gonna do with this pumpkin, Ms. Rager?" Tyler asked as he sat next to her at the kitchen table.

She sat so that her knee touched his, awareness crawling up her body. The look in his eyes showed her that he felt it as well. "I dunno, I've always been kinda traditional and simple. Ya know, the triangles for the eyes and nose and some craziness for the mouth."

"Well, we can do that, or you can let me do it," his voice deepened as he looked at the pumpkin thoughtfully.

"Let him do it," Liam advised.

"Why should I do that?" she asked, a bright smile on her face.

"Cause homeboy over there can draw and carve like you wouldn't believe."

A blush rose on Tyler's cheeks and she looked at him, surprise on her face. "You can?"

"A little bit," he shrugged.

Liam snorted. "Don't let him fool you, he's really modest about it. C'mere." He crooked his finger, and she got up to follow him.

He led them through the house, staying a respectable distance away from her, aware that she was still a little jumpy around men. When they got to the living room, he pointed to a charcoal drawing that hung over a fireplace that had been carved into the wall. The scene depicted a Native American woman holding her child on the plains. Her long hair blew in the breeze and the sadness in her eyes radiated out to whomever looked at it. No detail went unnoticed as tears almost came to her eyes.

"He did that?"

Liam nodded. "Yeah, he's really talented."

The things she kept finding out about this man who was committed to helping her made it very hard to keep her feelings compartmentalized. He was so much more than he appeared to be, and she just hoped that she would be enough for him. She never wanted to disappoint him.

Hours later, the group sat out on the screened in back porch at Liam and Denise's, admiring the pumpkins they'd carved. Meredith had taken Liam's advice and given Tyler free rein. What he had done was creepy, yet beautiful. It looked like a scarier version of the grim reaper. The two women sat sipping wine while the men nursed beers. Quiet conversation flowed easily between them.

"Are you going to dress up for the party?" Denise asked Meredith, when a lull in the conversation carried on for a few moments.

"The Halloween party? I dunno. After what happened the other day, I was thinking of totally skipping it."

"Oh c'mon, you can't skip it. We'll have a rule that no ski masks or hoodies can be worn," Denise told her.

"What happened the other day?" Tyler asked, his tone sharper than even he would have liked it to be. What had she not told him? When she held things back from him it pissed him off royally and he had to fight with himself to keep his temper in check. There wasn't anything he wouldn't do for this woman, and the fact that she wasn't truthful with her feelings flew all over him.

Meredith groaned. She hadn't told him about this for a reason. She didn't want him to get all bent out of shape. Plus, she'd never shared with him what the man who attacked her had worn. The only person she'd ever shared details with was her therapist, save for what she had to tell Ashley, the doctor who examined her afterwards.

"Sorry," Denise mouthed.

"When we went grocery shopping, a kid was wearing a ski mask and a black hoodie. He was just trying out his Halloween costume, but it hit me the wrong way," she tried to downplay the event.

"Because that's what *he* wore?" he asked, his eyes flashing brightly. His mind worked overtime, absorbing this new bit of information she had inadvertently let leak. She didn't know he went around at night or even during the day looking for men who gave him a feeling. Trying to see if he could find someone who would dare hurt his woman. He wanted revenge so badly his back teeth ached as he clenched them tightly together.

"Yes. Now I'd rather not talk about it anymore. That's what my therapy sessions are for."

For the first time, he dared argue with her. "I wish you'd tell me what happened. That way I could find him and cut his heart out. I know if you'd just give me a couple of clues, I could find the bastard. I could take care of it for you if you'd just fuckin' trust me enough."

The ice in his tone scared her. She wanted the man dead, but she didn't want it at the expense of Tyler's self-control. Many times she had watched him grapple with his temper, trying to keep it at a reasonable level for her. If he let his control go, who knew what he could do to the man that had hurt her?

"It's not about trusting you, it's about being able to talk about it. If you can't already tell that I trust you with my life, then you need to take a good hard look at what we're doing here. I'll share it when I'm ready to and not before," she whispered.

He realized that he had gone completely alpha male on her, and it looked like it had scared her. Forcing himself to release the tension from his body, he smiled as easily as possible at her. "I know, I'm sorry. I just want to take care of this for you. I'll be patient."

She knew he would be, and since this was the first time he'd lost his cool out loud, she would overlook it. "I know you will," she reached out her hand as a gesture of goodwill and placed it in his.

When she flipped her palm over, he ran his long fingers over the sensitive skin there and her breathing quickened. At this moment, for once, she wished her body and her mind would be on the same page.

Chapter Seven

This had been a bad idea, Meredith realized as soon as she made her way out to the packed main room of the clubhouse. It hadn't been hard to get up the hallway that led to the dorm rooms where most of the other members slept. Some of them had homes, some of them didn't. Those who didn't made their homes here. It was important that their private space be respected, so not a lot of people congregated in that tight spot. The main room was a completely different story. Everything had been pushed to the side – except for couches, where she could see a lot more people congregating than she was comfortable with.

The party was in full swing, and there were a ton of bodies packed into a very small space. She couldn't even bring herself to wear a costume, but a part of her had wanted to be among the action. She wanted to see what she was missing out on. Her eyes scanned the sea of bodies and locked with William's, who smiled warmly at her and saluted her with his beer. She smiled back, thankful that he had seen her in distress and offered her a friendly gesture.

"Meredith," Denise yelled from the edge of the crowd.

Making her way over to her friend, Meredith tried not to let people she didn't know touch her. "Hey, you look great," she complimented.

Denise wore a wizard outfit that included fake glasses and a wand.

"Thanks. Liam said something about me being a very naughty schoolgirl later on," she giggled, her eyes glassy with the alcohol she'd already consumed.

That hit Meredith in the stomach like a ton of bricks. What she wouldn't give for the carefree way Denise talked about and displayed her sexuality. "Well, you have a good time," she muttered.

"I'm gonna tell you somethin' and I don't want you to get mad at me." The drinks she had made her accent thicker, Meredith had to concentrate on listening to her.

"Okay."

"You need to stake your claim."

"What?" Meredith didn't understand her drunken ramblings.

"Women. They are all over Tyler tonight. You need to stake your damn claim."

Dread rolled in her stomach. "How? I can't even let the man touch me."

Denise sobered almost completely in that moment. "Have you tried?"

Sometimes her friend pissed her off with her honest questions. Meredith wasn't sure how it'd happened, but the two of them knew each other so well. She'd never had a friend like Denise who challenged her and wasn't afraid to call her on her bullshit.

"Where is he?" she asked through clenched teeth. This pissed her off. He was hers, even if she couldn't show him that yet.

"Follow the trail of scantily clad women, and he's at the end."

That was exactly what she hadn't wanted to hear. "Seriously. Can you just tell me where he is?"

Denise grabbed her hand, maneuvering them through the crowd. Up ahead, she could see a group of women, Tyler in the middle. He had a small smile on his face, obviously enjoying the attention. Meredith looked down at the loose jeans and huge shirt she wore.

"I look like a fucking soccer mom," she hissed at Denise. Her voice was thick with unshed tears and embarrassment. How had she let herself go? "I can't go up there like this. They'll laugh me out of the room."

"Then do something about it. I know you have it in you. I'm not telling you to have sex with him tonight, but you have got to stop stringing him along."

Meredith knew that she was right. He deserved so much more than she was able to give him. "You're right, but what am I going to wear?"

"Come with me."

It had taken them forever to get through the crowd and back to the dorm room that Liam used on occasion. Denise stumbled through the door after she'd fought to open it with her key.

"You need to take a break from the booze friend of mine. You won't be able to be a naughty school girl later on if you can't keep from puking."

"That's good advice, now I'm going to give you some. Wear this out there. Forget your insecurities, inhibitions, and fear for a little while. Take it minute by minute, and I think you'll be fine. I picked this up for you, hoping that jealously would make you lay claim on that man."

Denise threw a bag on the bed along with some makeup products and shoes.

"How sexy is it?" Meredith asked, her breath already starting to become more rapid in her chest.

"Just calm down. You aren't showing anything except your legs and chest. I promise you, it's not too risqué at all."

When she was dressed, Meredith turned around in the mirror, checking herself from all sides. She had to admit that Denise had been right. A fairy costume hadn't been what she was expecting, so she forewent the wings that were supposed to go on her back. While it was sexy, it was also modest. A white corset inlaid in a dress pushed her breasts up, but not indecently so. White tights covered her legs and a white mask over her eyes showed only the eye makeup she wore. The skirt came down right to her knees, and the white heels she wore made her legs look exceptionally long. The contrast of the white clothes she wore against her dark hair that she'd curled and pulled back was striking.

"Wow," she breathed, getting another glimpse at herself.

"Do you feel comfortable?" Denise asked. "Because if you don't, I won't make you do this." She wanted to make her do it, but she wouldn't.

Meredith could see the excitement in Denise's eyes. Her friend wanted her to take back a part of herself. "Ya know what? I do."

"Then go out there and get your man. Here, take a shot before you go, you might need it."

Meredith coughed as the vanilla flavored vodka burned on its way down, but it steadied her shaking hands. Before going out the door, she hugged Denise fiercely. "Thank you."

"You don't have to thank me at all. You're doin' this all on your own. I just gave you the tools."

As she rejoined the party, Meredith noticed that it had gotten a little louder, a little wilder, and a little raunchier. With new determination she made her way through the crowd, not even shrinking away when someone pressed against her that she didn't know. Out of nowhere, William came up behind her and put an arm out, keeping others away.

"You're my knight in shining armour tonight," she grinned.

"Just trying to be of service to my brother," he winked at her. It was unusual for him to be in such a jovial mood, but she wrote it off as the alcohol he'd probably consumed.

She was on a mission this time. The group of women around Tyler had grown bigger, and one woman stood a little too close for Meredith's comfort. Squaring her shoulders, she marched right up to them and stood where the women couldn't help but see her.

He hadn't been paying attention, talking to Liam who stood off to the side, conveniently ignoring every woman who walked up to him. She cleared her throat loudly, causing him to look at her. When he did, her inner self smiled brightly at the surprise in his eyes. His pupils darkened almost immediately.

"Meredith?" he stammered, giving her a once over.

"Yeah, I thought I'd come out here and give you a break, looks like you have a little bit too much *company*."

Holy shit, she's jealous, he thought. What an interesting turn of events this was. "They aren't wanted."

"I know. You're just too nice to tell them that."

She saddled up to his side and pushed the girl who had been too close for comfort out of the way. He immediately turned into her, blocking her body from everyone else's view.

"This is nice," he indicated the outfit that she wore, running a finger down her cheek and along the side of her body.

She closed her eyes, relishing the feel of his touch.

"It's sexy," he told her, bringing his lips close to her ear so that she could hear him over the magnitude of the crowd.

She shivered, bringing her hands up to his biceps to keep herself from swaying on her heels. His voice, so deep and smooth, swept over her.

"It was Denise's idea."

He chuckled low in his throat. "Remind me to thank her. Then remind me to thank these women who've been on my nerves all night. They obviously made you jealous."

"I couldn't help it," she admitted, glancing up into his eyes.

They stood that way for a long moment, his face tilted towards hers, staring into each other's eyes. His big hands spanned her waist, and he brought them up to rest on her back.

"I'd like to kiss you," he warned her.

"I think I would like that," she answered back, breathless.

The spell broke between them as he glanced around and noticed the group of women glaring at her. "Not here, follow me."

He grabbed her hand and dragged her along the outskirts of the party, opening a door to the garage where bikes that were being worked on were kept. They were alone, and she could hear her breath echoing off the emptiness of the room.

"Is this okay?" he asked her softly, not knowing how she felt about being alone with him while the atmosphere between them was so sexually charged.

"More than," she told him and realized it was the truth.

Slowly, he brought his hands up to her cheeks and framed them. His big thumbs stroked the skin there, feeling how hot they were.

"Embarrassed or aroused?" he asked, indicating the blush that had formed there.

"A little bit of both," she admitted shakily.

"I'm not gonna force you to do something you don't want to do. So if you want this, you've gotta come to me."

She realized that in his own way he was making her tell him what she wanted, and while a part of her hated it, another part of her rejoiced. Placing her hands on his waist under his cut, she fisted his shirt in them and pulled their bodies closer together. He groaned as she tilted her head opposite his and fused their lips together. His hands remained on her cheeks, not exerting any pressure, letting her control the kiss. She pulled back, then went forward, peppering little kisses on his lips, getting used to the feel of him.

"Thank you," she whispered, as she leaned into his body, hugging him to her.

"Whatever you need, whatever you want, I'm here," he promised. "But I need you to let me know what that is."

She clung to him, tears coming to her eyes, and in an instant, they sprang free.

"Shh," he comforted, running his hands through her hair. "Let it all out," he instructed her.

With the tears that flowed, Meredith let go of a dam on the emotions that held her back. It cleansed her body and her mind, allowing her to really feel for the first time since the attack. He held her as she broke down and knew that he'd never be able to let her go.

Chapter Eight

Meredith breathed heavily as she did her second lap around the Heaven Hill compound. The kiss the night before had opened a flood of emotions within her, and she hadn't been able to sleep very long once they'd made their way back to Tyler's dorm room. She'd lain there tossing and turning most of the night, thoughts racing through her head. Usually running helped, but not even the steady pounding of her shoes on the ground cleared her thoughts today. Stopping when she finally had a stitch in her side, she bent over. Panting, she crossed her hands above her head and began slowing walking around.

"You okay?" Denise asked as she walked up beside the other woman.

"Fine," she panted, although her eyes betrayed her. "You?"

Her friend decided to let the obvious lie go and smiled dreamily. "It was an amazing night once we got home. Have I mentioned how hot Liam is? How much I love him? How we decided to maybe try and have a baby?"

The water that Meredith had just taken a sip of spit forward out of her mouth. "Come again?"

"Yeah," she beamed. "We talked about it, and we decided that since I'm still young and he wants to, we're gonna try and have a baby."

The enthusiasm that she tried to show froze in her throat. This had been her dream, having a husband and a child. Jealously reared its ugly head and Meredith had to hit it with all her might to push it down. "That's great. I'm so happy for you!"

Denise smiled sadly at her friend. "No you're not, this is something you want. Isn't it?"

"I'm in no position to know what I want at this point," she argued.

"It's okay to not be thrilled for us, seriously," Denise soothed.

Meredith leaned against the chain link fence that surrounded the compound and put her face in her hands. "You're right, I want all of that," she whispered, tears coming to her eyes.

The hollow feeling that settled in the pit of her stomach made her want to puke. It angered her and frustrated her, but at the same time gave her such a feeling of despair. She tried so hard to keep it together, not to let Denise know how much this affected her, but it was futile. The tears came and she couldn't stop them. Gut wrenching sobs exploded from her chest, and the complete devastation she felt shattered her.

Not knowing what to do, Denise grabbed her shoulders and pulled her close for a hug. It shocked her when Meredith buried her head in the other woman's shoulder and hung on for dear life. Maybe this is what she'd been missing. The human contact, the feeling of someone else physically helping her hold herself together.

"Talk to me," Denise pleaded. "You're not going to hurt my feelings one bit. Tell me how you're feeling."

Her nose ran and Meredith coughed as she shook her head, trying to clear the tears from her eyes. "Devastated. I feel like all my dreams are gone," her broken voice cracked and the sobs started over again.

"They're not, honey. Now's the time to realize those dreams, make new ones."

Someone who hadn't had such things taken from them couldn't understand, and Meredith couldn't seem to explain it with enough detail that others knew where she was coming from. She felt so alone.

"I'm broken and I just don't know if I can ever be fixed," she whimpered as she curled her fingers around Denise's shoulders and hung on for dear life.

"You're gonna be fixed. I won't allow you not to be," Denise vowed, rocking the other woman as she cried it all out.

"What happened?" Tyler barked as Meredith made her way back into the clubhouse.

She looked like death warmed over. Her eyes were red rimmed and puffy, her face a sick white pallor. The woman in front of him looked ready to collapse.

"I really don't wanna talk about it," she croaked out. Her throat was raw with all the crying she'd done, and she was physically exhausted. For the first time in months it felt like she could go to sleep and stay there for days. It had finally caught up with her, the utter exhaustion that she'd been feeling. Perhaps it was really depression and it'd finally just overtaken her body.

Tyler fought back the protective side he had for her and did his best to respect her wishes. She walked slowly to his dorm room, and he followed her at a respectable distance, hoping not to spook her.

"Anything I can do for you?" he asked softly.

Frustration and anger made her lash out. "I'm so *sick* of people doing things for me. Treating me like I can't do anything for myself. It drives me crazy," she screamed.

Taken aback, he didn't say anything, just listened to her rage.

"Poor Meredith, she got raped and she can't sleep at night and nothing is ever going to be the same for her again. Let's treat her with kid gloves and keep her from getting too stressed out because she might have a nervous breakdown."

He herded her into the dorm room and shut the door. "Are you done?"

"No, I'm not done. I'm so sick of this."

She charged into him and screamed, pushing him back against the door to the room. He didn't try to hold her arms back, just let her go as she started to beat her fists into his chest. After several long minutes, she stopped, collapsing against him.

Carefully, he put his arms around her, hugging her to him. She launched her arms around his neck, holding on for dear life, and it took him by surprise. She was so tentative usually when she touched other people.

"Please, don't let me go," she begged tearfully. It was there, the need for human touch. It was finally there again.

"I won't," he promised. "I will be here for as long as you need. For whatever you need me for. I'm not gonna let you down."

She knew without a doubt that he was telling the truth. She also knew that in order for them to move forward, she was going to have to get uncomfortable. Try things that she hadn't before and put her fears aside. If she could have him and everything she wanted though, it would be worth every single drop of fear, anxiety, and sadness she'd ever felt.

Chapter Nine

I am a hot mess. I completely went off on Tyler and Denise yesterday. I embarrassed myself beyond belief, and the truth is, I'm not sure whether it did any good or not. I still have so many emotions and thoughts running through my head. I just don't know how to get them all out, how to let go of these feelings that keep eating me up from the inside out. I had a breakthrough though. I realized I need it. I need human touch. I want Tyler to hug me, his finger to brush my cheek, I want him to hold me while I sleep.

Meredith put down her journal and bit her thumbnail thoughtfully. Last night had been the first night of real sleep she'd gotten since this whole ordeal had started. Why, she wasn't sure, but thought maybe she'd reached a turning point, and perhaps the emotions of the last few days had finally gotten to her. For the first time when she'd woken up this morning, she believed that she would come through this on the other side. Not unscathed, but possibly able to enjoy her life. To be able to get married and have children and have what others would consider a normal life. She even thought that maybe she would be able to have that with Tyler. But before she would be able to do that, she had to come to grips with her mental issues. That's why she'd made another appointment with her therapist, sooner than normal.

She placed her journal in its safe spot and then went to find Tyler. She found him at the kitchen table with Liam, drinking from his ever present skull mug.

"Morning," he greeted her, offering a small smile.

She knew that she didn't deserve that. Not really. Not after the way she'd acted the night before and the blubbering mess she'd been before assaulting him. But she'd take it.

"Morning. Do you think that you and your skull mug can take me to a doctor's appointment here in a few?"

His brows narrowed. "Something wrong?"

"No, I just feel like after last night, I need to talk about some stuff."

He realized that she didn't really want to get into it with Liam around and, thankfully, he didn't press her for further info. "Let me just wash my cup and then we can jet."

Jagger, a new member of the club who was just coming out of his Prospect period, stopped him. "Nah, man, I got it. You go on."

Movement in the club stopped. Everyone watched as Jagger grinned and picked up the mug, showing what he considered proper respect for his elder officer. He took it over to the sink, washed and dried it quickly before bringing it back to the table and setting it down in front of Tyler. It wasn't until then that he noticed all eyes on him.

"What?" he asked, uncomfortable with the stares that followed him. Even Liam looked at him, mouth hanging wide open. "You never seen somebody pay some respect to somebody else and do a dish?"

"I haven't ever seen anybody touch that mug, including me," Liam clarified, watching Jagger with wide eyes. "Tyler always hints that it's cursed, but he never tells us for sure."

Finally picking up on what he was saying, Jagger lost his swagger and looked at Tyler. "The fuck man? Seriously? Is it cursed?"

"I guess you'll just have to find out, won't you?"

"I'm ready to move on," Meredith told Dr. Jones with such determination in her voice even she believed it.

"What does that mean?"

"It means I want to try and get physical again. I want to get married, I want to have children. I want this to stop hanging over my head. I want to take my life back."

"I caution you again, Meredith, not to rush yourself. Don't do this out of some misguided sense that there's a timeline."

She shook her head. "I'm not. I let Tyler kiss me the other night."

"How did that go?"

"Pretty well. I think if he had tried, I would have let him go further."

Something in her eyes caused the Doctor to sit forward and regard her seriously. "What brought this on, and be honest with me."

"My friend Denise and her old man, boyfriend, whatever, have decided to have a baby," Meredith sighed. "This is what I wanted for so long, and I feel like the world is just moving on without me."

"Nothing moves on without you, Meredith. Your world goes at your pace, theirs goes at theirs."

"And trust me, I know that, but I'm just sick of Tyler sleeping on the floor. If you get what I mean."

A patient smile appeared on Doctor Jones' face. "You really think you're ready for that?"

"I think I'm getting there, but I'm not sure how not to freak out."

Doctor Jones thought over her words carefully and very softly suggested her regimen of therapy. "Masturbation."

"What?" Meredith coughed, her face flaming red.

"You have to get comfortable with sexual feelings and touches again. What better way to do that than for you to have complete control over what you're doing. He can even watch."

"The hell he will," she shouted.

"You've never done that before?"

Something about the older woman asking her that caused Meredith to giggle and then she couldn't stop. "Are you a freak under those professional clothes, Doc?"

"Two consenting adults watching each other masturbate does not a freak make," she smiled, not really answering the question.

Meredith could see where the doctor was coming from and was sure that she'd used this method of treatment with other rape survivors before, but she honestly knew nothing about what the doctor was asking her to do. "Where do I even begin?"

"Tell Tyler to take you to Upton," she smiled mysteriously.

"What's in Upton?"

"Trust me, Tyler knows and he won't even question it. Just walk out that door, tell him to take you there, and I'd like to see you in the next couple of days."

Armed with her new 'homework' fresh in her brain, Meredith walked out, a bemused look on her face. Tyler had a cell phone to his ear and was grinning in an evilly wicked way she'd never seen before. Holding up his finger, he continued talking for a few moments before ending the call.

"Everything alright?" she asked when he doubled over with laughter.

"Jagger ran into a chair and broke his toe. The 'curse of the skull' is in full effect."

She couldn't tell if he was joking or not.

"Seriously, is that damn thing cursed or not?"

"What do you think?" he asked her with a quirked brow.

The fact of the matter was, she just wasn't sure. Jagger was making a good case for it being cursed though. "I don't know still. I'll reserve judgment for a later date. Now I have a favor to ask."

"What's that?" he asked, leaning against the bike. His long legs crossed at the ankle and his hands rested at his sides. She loved how comfortable he was in his body. A small amused smile still played at the edges of his lips.

"Can you take me to Upton?"

His eyes darkened and that smile turned sexy, transforming his face. "You sure?"

"Yeah. Doc Jones told me to ask you to take me there. I'm not sure what's there, but she said it was crucial to my recovery."

He hopped on the bike and patted the seat behind him for her. Once she got on and put her arms around him, he turned his face into hers and quickly connected their lips. "This, baby, is going to be my complete pleasure."

Chapter Ten

Meredith couldn't help the smile that spread across her face as she and Tyler made their way north up I-65. Being with him on a bike was quickly becoming her very favorite place to be. As he wove in and out of traffic, she enjoyed the scenery. A few years before, a major ice storm had destroyed most of the brush and trees along the interstate, but they were beginning to make a comeback. Given the time of year and the fact they'd had plenty of rain, the colors were beautiful. Gripping his waist, she took the moment to lean her head against his back and just breathe.

It felt like this every time.

She could breathe with him around. She could let down her guard and not worry that someone would hurt her. It was nice, relaxing, and freeing. His presence seemed to be the only relief she could get from the jittery, nervous feelings that constantly resided in her stomach.

Watching the miles tick away, she glanced at the next green sign that indicated how far they were away from certain destinations in Kentucky. This particular one showed Upton to be only a few miles up the road. Her stomach gave a lurch, but this time not in fear, in excitement.

As the bike ate up the miles, she noticed a sign up ahead proclaiming Jesus saved. She raised her eyebrows as Tyler took that exit and slowed down the bike. A stop sign at the end of the road told they could go either left or right, he chose right and then hung another right at the next road. It looked like they were in the middle of nowhere and her curiosity was piqued. They passed a gas station and a run-down motel before pulling into a parking lot where the back side of the building proclaimed this was a sex shop that was open 24/7 including Christmas Day.

He parked the bike and turned it off, getting off it as he gauged her reaction carefully.

"A sex store?"

The grin that came to his face looked like it couldn't be helped. "Tell me exactly what your therapist said to you, because I'm intrigued. By the way, you'll need your ID."

She took the moment to glance down into the saddle bag that she stowed her stuff in, fishing out her ID. It gave her just enough time to get the redness in her face under control. This was so far out of her element that she wanted to run screaming.

"Masturbation," she mumbled.

This grin was shit eating. "Well, we've come to the right place, sweetheart. After you," he ushered her into the store.

Once inside, she did her best not to let her eyes pop out of her head. It was sensory overload at its finest. Before they could pass into the main store, a man requested both their ID's and ticked them off with a ticker he held in his hand. The smile he gave Tyler made her blood curl just a little.

"You come here often?" she hissed.

"I'm not gonna lie. I'm a red-blooded male. I been here a few times."

That was so not what she wanted to hear. Had he come here with other women? Had they eagerly picked out toys to use and videos to watch and then gone back to his dorm room and put them all to use? It took the shine off the experience.

"I've never been here with another woman, if that's what you're wondering."

He could always read what she felt, could always see inside her head, and she needed it so bad sometimes. "Thanks for not makin' me ask that."

"I could tell you were interested."

An awkward beat passed between the two of them, and she had to look away from his face. Sometimes the intensity she saw there was too much for her to handle.

"So what am I looking at here?"

Tyler looked at her, eyebrows raised. "You don't know? You never been in one of these stores or to any of your girlfriend's parties?"

"Let's just say I've never really had that many girlfriends, and no I've never been to a store like this before."

He knew that this next question would be very uncomfortable for her, so he leaned in as close as he could. It was so close his hair brushed her shoulder and his lips lightly touched her ear. "Please tell me you've masturbated before."

She immediately tensed up and he took a step back. "No, I didn't tense because you were that close to me, that was actually nice. I tensed up because of well, you know, the other thing," her face flashed a hot red.

"You are twenty-four years old, how can you be embarrassed about this?" he laughed, putting an arm around her neck and pulling her close.

Meredith buried her head in his chest and blew out a deep breathe, collecting herself. "This just isn't who I am, I've never been really good at dealing with this stuff. It's always embarrassed me. I grew up in a home where sex wasn't discussed."

Come to think of it, not much was discussed in her home besides the fact she needed to go to college and make something of herself. Her family wasn't well off, but they didn't lack for anything. None of them had been good at showing their feelings, which was probably why now she preferred just to stay away. It was easier than trying to make her parents feel something that she wasn't ever sure had been there.

"Well we're gonna discuss it. We're gonna start with what the therapist said you need to be doin'. So let's go over to this wall right here."

He steered her to a wall of brightly colored vibrators and other female sex toys.

"Just pick me something out," she moaned.

Putting his hand on her chin, he turned her around so that he could see in her eyes and she could see in his. "This has to be you, Meredith. You have to decide what you're going to do here. Do you want to heal or do you want to be stuck in the same place you are right now. If I pick this out for you, then he's still won because you won't embrace your femininity."

Tears sprung to her eyes. All of a sudden, it made sense. Doctor Jones had wanted Tyler to bring her here because he got it. He knew that she needed to be pushed, but in a positive way. He encouraged her to make her own decisions and accomplish her own victories. "You're right. Thank you for this."

"Now if you want me here while you do this, I'll be here. If you don't want me here, I'll go over to the men's section. It's up to you."

Again he gave her the space to make her own decision.

"I think I wanna do this on my own," she whispered.

Tyler nodded and leaned down, kissing her on the forehead. "I'll be right over there if you need me."

When he left, she stood gazing at the wall. It was so overwhelming, the amount of options she had to choose from. Part of her wanted to grab them and feel of them, but she was too shy. Pushing her hair behind her ears, she gnawed on her bottom lip in thought.

"You can pick them up if you want you know?" the man who'd checked her ID when she'd come in had come up behind her, obviously ready to make a sale.

Her hands and voice shaking, she took that leap forward. "I just don't really know what I want."

The salesman reached around her and picked up one of the smaller models and held it out to her. "Do you like the way this feels? It's small, but powerful. If you don't care about the girth, then I've had a lot of women come back and tell me they love this. Now if it's something like a real dick you want, you'll want one of those bigger ones over there. All vibrate, but some of them have more features than the other. If this if your first time in a shop like this, then I recommend you get two instead of one. Get two completely opposite of each other, that way you can really find out what you like. Don't be scared to pick them up and get a feel of them. They won't bite."

His candidness was exactly what she needed. He smiled at her as he talked, engaging her in the conversation. It made her feel like she wasn't the only woman who'd ever been at a shop like this, doing what she was doing. It was everything she'd hoped for when she made this journey.

After she'd selected what she wanted, she and Tyler walked up to the checkout and she hid her head in Tyler's chest again as the salesman tested the products to make sure they worked.

Tyler and the salesman had a good rapport and teased her good naturedly. The smile on her face was one of the first that had seemed genuine since her attack. After everything was in the bag, Tyler pulled out cash to pay for her purchases.

"No, Ty," she tried to push at his hand. Funny, she'd never felt comfortable enough with him to have a nickname before, but she did now. Maybe this trip had done more for her than even the good doctor had figured.

He pushed her hand out of the way. "Let me do this for you."

She could see in his eyes how much he wanted to do it and she grinned, letting him know it was okay. As they left the store, the smile stayed on her face.

"That smile is a good look on you," he commented as they made their way to his bike.

"This smile is one hundred percent because of you, Tyler Blackfoot."

That statement warmed his heart more than anything else had in a very long time.

"What do you say? Get me home and I can try this stuff out?"

Her flirtiness surprised him, but if she felt comfortable then he would not discourage her. "Whatever you feel like, baby."

As they hopped on the bike, she thought about what he'd said. For the first time in a long time she felt sexy, dangerous, wild, wanton, and like an improved version of herself. She realized that she felt like a woman who wanted to seduce her man. She wasn't sure if she could go through with it or not, but just having the want was enough for her.

Chapter Eleven

An hour later, the two of them pulled up to an old farmhouse that she'd never seen before. It was charming, with a tin roof that looked like it'd been recently replaced, but the paint peeled off the sides of the weather beaten house. He turned the bike off and threw his long leg over the side.

"What's this place?" she asked.

"It's mine. It's my refuge when I need time to myself."

That was news to her. She'd never heard anyone talk about Tyler having a home of his own, and he'd sure never said anything about it. Her reporter's mind had a ton of questions. Inquisitive for the first time since the attack.

"I can see the questions in your eyes, but can you respect that I really just don't wanna talk about it right now."

He'd respected everything about her situation, and she realized for the first time that she wasn't the same person she'd been before. The types of questions that sprung to her mind now weren't the ones she'd had before. These were much more humane, they were more about the person than the story. She didn't feel that obsessive need to know the answers to the questions that sprung to mind.

Instead she wanted to wait for him to tell her, not bully or trick him into an answer.

"Whenever you wanna talk about it, we can. I won't pressure you. You have my promise on that."

Taking her hand, he led her into the house and flipped on the living room light. It was surprisingly clean, very much a bachelor pad. A huge sectional couch was the only piece of furniture besides a large screen plasma TV. A gazillion video games systems were hooked up to it and a large wooden case held DVD's.

"Not much, I know, but it's mine."

She glimpsed regret and possibly embarrassment in his eyes. "No, not at all, I'm just taking it all in. This is so much different than your dorm room."

"Well c'mon, I'll give you the tour."

Comfortably, she put her hand in his again, and he led her through the house. He showed her the kitchen, the bathroom, a spare room that he obviously did a lot of painting in, and then his bedroom.

"This is the room I've done the most work to."

She cocked her head to the side. "So you're remodeling?"

"You could say that."

He opened the door to his bedroom and she gasped. New carpet covered the floor, thick and plush. She immediately wanted to take off her shoes and sink into it. Three walls were painted a dark gray and one was covered in what looked like restored boards. His bed was larger than any she'd ever seen. It had to be custom made, given how tall he was. A chair sat in the corner with an ottoman along with a chest of drawers. She saw a picture on the chest of drawers and wondered immediately who it was. She'd never seen a picture at his dorm, and he'd never been one to pull one out of his wallet.

"This is gorgeous," she breathed. "That wall is amazing, what kind of boards are those?"

"There was an old barn behind the house, over a hundred years old. When I decided to tear it down, I decided to re-purpose the boards. I refinished them and used them on the wall. Eventually, I want to add a bathroom in here, but that's gonna take more money than I've got right now."

It filled him with pride that she'd said the room was gorgeous. He was proud of the work he'd done, and it warmed his heart that she seemed to like it too. When he'd first started remodeling this house, it had been for himself only, but he could quickly see it being for her as well.

"I'm sure that no matter what you do, it's going to be amazing."

He turned to face her, bringing his hand up to her jaw. "Do you really have that much faith in me?" his voice was hoarse as he asked the question.

"I do, Tyler. You've had so much faith in me that I can't help to return that to you. If we support each other, there's nothing we can't do."

Bending down, he took the bag she'd held in her hand since they'd gotten off the bike and set it on the chair in the corner. "I have faith in you that you can do this," he told her.

Her mind swam, was she supposed to do this on her own? Was he supposed to watch? Would he want to watch? Would she want him to watch?

"Hey, don't freak out on me," he calmly stroked her hair. "What do you want me to do?"

"I don't know," she sniffed, tears coming to her eyes.

This was not what he'd wanted. He didn't want her to tense up so much that she wouldn't or couldn't enjoy what she'd been so set on doing before. Decision made, he stood in front of her, spreading his legs so that he was almost eye level with her and cupped her face in his large hands. Forcing her to look into his eyes, he spoke slowly and concisely so that she would understand every word.

"If I do something you don't want me to do, you tell me. No matter what. I don't want you to feel uncomfortable, but we have to be honest with each other here. Why don't you go take a hot shower and relax? I'll be here waiting for you when you're ready."

She let the tears spill over her eyes and nodded slowly. He left her, going over to the chest of drawers and pulled out a shirt.

"You can wear this."

Taking it, she left the bedroom and went to the bathroom, her smile tremulous. As she cranked the hot water, she took a deep breath. Without a doubt, this would make or break their relationship, and regardless of what the outcome was, she knew she had to at least attempt to get through it. Squaring her shoulders, she stepped inside the shower and willed herself to relax.

After Meredith left, Tyler let out a breath he didn't know he'd been holding. He was scared to death that she'd run screaming. He felt things for this woman he'd never felt for another human being before – ever. It was damn scary, and he wasn't sure he was even equipped to handle it, much less deal with it. Pulling out his cell phone, he texted Liam to let him know that he would be off the grid for a couple days at the most. The protection runs he'd been tapped to participate in would have to wait. He knew mentioning Meredith would get him an immediate out. In the time she'd been at the clubhouse, she'd gotten under everyone's skin, regardless of how she'd started out.

When he got the affirming text that told him that everything was taken care of, he turned the phone off and set it on top of the dresser. Taking off his cut, he put it on the chair and went to work taking off his motorcycle boots. Quickly he disarmed himself, putting his gun within reach, but where Meredith wouldn't be likely to spy it and stowing the knife he also carried in the drawer of the bedside table. Like most of his brothers, he wore a ring on his hand that read HH, and he took that off as well. When he'd disrobed himself as much as he dared, he had a seat on the bed and propped himself up against the pillows that lay there. Feigning an air of disinterest he didn't really feel, he waited.

After an hour, he wondered if Meredith would really be able to go through with this and was getting up to tell her that she didn't have to when he heard the door to the bathroom open. Putting his hands behind his head, he waited anxiously.

"You alright?" he yelled when she didn't appear for a few moments.

"Close your eyes," she instructed.

He couldn't help but grin and close his eyes as she asked. "They're closed."

Meredith stepped into the doorway of the bedroom and bit her lip, she wondered if he thought her too forward. But she'd come to the conclusion in the shower if she was going to do this, she was going to have to do it right. "Okay, open 'em!"

"Holy shit," he whispered. She stood there, naked as the day she was born.

Chapter Twelve

She had to give it him, he lay on the bed with his arms behind his head, never once flinching as she walked towards him.

"Whatever you feel comfortable with," he reminded her.

She'd taken the time in the shower to shave and do all the things she'd hadn't felt the need to do in the past weeks since her attack. She'd found some girly shampoo and body wash and had treated herself like she'd been at a spa. It had been on the tip of her tongue to ask if the girly stuff had been for her or if he'd had another woman at this place before, but she didn't want to ruin the mood.

Her hands shook as she made her way over to where he lay. Her brain screamed at her to run the other way and never look back, but she knew that she had to do this. She knew that she couldn't let this defeat her anymore.

"You're beautiful," he whispered.

The smile that came to her face was so genuine it made him want to cry. It seemed to give her the push she needed. Without hesitation that he had suspected, she lifted herself over his body and straddled him. It surprised her how much she wanted his hands on her, but she knew that unless she told him or showed him, he wouldn't touch her. Placing her hands on his shoulders she situated herself on his lap to make sure she wouldn't fall.

Once comfortable, she leaned forward and put her mouth on his, kissing him with everything she felt. Of its own violition, her tongue plundered his mouth, getting swept up in the feel of their bodies against each other. His taste was an aphrodisiac. He always tasted of coffee and tobacco, even though she'd never seen him smoke. With other men, it would have been a turn off, on him it was sweet and earthy. Reaching behind his head, she put her hands on his and directed them to her breasts, conforming them around the globes that dangled without the restraint of a bra.

"Please," she whimpered.

His long fingers massaged the aching flesh as she put her arms around his neck and pressed their bodies closer together. The hardness of his manhood crushed against the wetness that was quickly building at her core. It felt good to her, better than it ever had before. She'd never had these kind of out of control feelings with any other man. It was quickly becoming out of hand, but she went with it. Maybe she wouldn't have to use those toys just yet – that's how wound up he made her.

"You feel so good," she told him, grinding her body against his.

He leaned forward, letting his lips trail down the column of her neck, leaving a wet line before he pushed himself forward enough to take a nipple into his mouth. She moaned loudly as his tongue swept over the hard tip, a caress all its own.

Meredith opened her eyes, watching him. He was just as beautiful as he made her feel. His long dark lashes were stark against his skin and the stain of arousal rose on his strong cheeks. His expression was intense as he worked her nipple with his tongue, using his teeth to nip gently. She shivered, fisting her hands in his hair, holding him tighter against her. With a mind of its own, his other hand went to where her bottom rocked against his cock, showing her the rhythm that he knew instinctively would get her off. He knew that if she was in the moment, she might be completely free to let herself go.

"What do you need me to do?" he asked, his voice rough.

The tone may have scared her if his touch wasn't still so soft and smooth. No matter what he had to be feeling, he still kept himself in check. She had figured that when she got this far into it, the crazy feeling of her body releasing its tension in orgasm, she might panic. It surprised her how badly she wanted it, how badly she wanted to experience the *little death* with this man.

"Just keep doing what you're doing, don't stop," she panted as she increased the speed of her hips against the hardness of his cock.

His body tightened as she panted with each lift of her hips, each grind of her pussy against him, he wanted this so badly for her. Her breath came faster and faster as she wound her arms tighter around his neck, using them to help the up and down motion.

"Give it to me, c'mon baby," he encouraged her.

Her nails cut into his neck so hard, he was sure she drew blood, but the bite of pain was fine with him. He held her body, strung tight as a bow as she fought for the orgasm that appeared to be just out of her reach. Frustration was beginning to take over, he could tell. It set just beyond the cusp of her reach. Her face screwed up, and he could see tears come to her eyes.

"Touch yourself," he instructed her. "Don't worry about me, get yourself off."

His deep voice was a caress against her skin, causing goose bumps to appear along her arms and legs. Before, she would have clammed up, embarrassed to do this in front of someone else, but she needed this *so* bad. Unclasping her hands from around his neck, she brought her finger to his mouth, pushing it against his lips. He swirled his tongue around it, sucking before letting it go with a loud pop. Hooded eyes met his as she took the finger and moved it down to the middle of her body. He could feel it, her finger strumming against her clit, and it made him hot, hotter than anything else ever had.

With a growl, he clamped his teeth and shut the door on his own needs. This was completely about her. He could feel her body tightening again as her finger increased its speed. Bringing his hands up around the back of her body, he dropped her back in a dip, closing his lips again around her nipple. The angle did it and he knew as soon as he shifted her that it did.

"Oh Tyler," she cried, the tension flowing from her body as she tightened her thighs around his hips.

"Give it to me," he instructed and held her as she rode it out.

When she was finally done, she collapsed against him, tears streaming down her face.

Chapter Thirteen

Tyler felt the warmth of the tears that Meredith continued to shed on his bare chest. She had immediately collapsed against him and had snuggled up so tightly to him, he didn't want to let her go. Even though she still cried, it had slowed considerably and her breathing had evened out, matching his.

"Thank you," she whispered, running the back of her hand across her nose.

"Hey," he caught her chin, tipping it so that he could look into her eyes. She felt his hand come up behind her head and tangle in her hair to keep her steady. "The pleasure was all mine. You are one hot piece of ass," he teased.

She gave a very unladylike snort that caused a smile to spread across his face. "I can still feel how hard you are," she wiggled against him.

"Doesn't matter," he shook his head. "This has been the most pleasure I've ever had. You let me worry about how hard I am."

That didn't sound fair to her, almost like he was taking something away that should be hers. "What if I wanted to help you, the way you helped me."

For the first time, panic flared in his eyes. "I think maybe this time, I should work this out on my own," he told her carefully, reaching down to adjust himself.

It was cute, as a smile curved along her face. Her eyes looked up to him and just like that she took on the role of seductress. "Do I at least get to watch?"

Good God, she was going to kill him. "If you want."

Untangling her body from his, she lay on her stomach facing him, obviously ready for a show.

"You're making me feel like I'm just a piece of meat," he joked as he stood up and took off his shirt.

"What a fine piece you are," she went right along with him. It was on the tip of her tongue to ask if she should run and get a dollar bill when it hit her right in the gut. Her attacker had thrown that dollar bill at her in disgust.

"You alright?" he asked, noticing her face lose its color.

This was important. This was one of those times in life when a conscious decision is made about your past and future. Would she continue to let her past affect her present, thereby affecting her future? She couldn't let it anymore and she knew she had to let it go.

"I'm fine. You just keep stripping your hot body bare," she whooped, hoping to cover up the misstep she'd just had.

He hadn't missed the dead look in her eye, the panic and despair that had resided there for just a split second. Whatever it was, he wouldn't question it and he'd do whatever she asked. He wondered if he had triggered her by accident and tucked that question in his pocket for a later time. He didn't need to know what it was, but he wanted to know if he did something involuntarily to cause her pain. Moving his hands to the button his jeans, he raised his eyebrows.

"You sure you can handle this?"

The teasing was everything she needed. Laughing she sat up on her knees. "Show me all you got."

He made a big show of taking his jeans off and throwing them on the chair next to his cut. The boxer briefs he wore underneath outlined his manhood well. She could tell he was gifted, hopefully he was talented to. When the time came for that. The little joke caused her to giggle.

"You're killin' me here baby. I'm strippin' and I'm down to my underwear and I'm hard as stone and you're laughin'? My self-esteem just took a huge nose dive."

His southern accent was much more pronounced now, a true indicator of just how turned on he was.

She shook her head, "Just a little joke I told myself. As big as you look, I realize you're gifted, but are you talented too?"

Taking off his underwear, he flicked it behind him and sauntered over to the bed. "I have no problem showing you just how talented I am at a later date," he promised, his large hand going to where his cock stood at attention.

She watched, not taking her eyes off his hand. When she'd told him that she wasn't very sexually experienced, she hadn't been lying. This was one of the things she'd never watched, never participated in. Embarrassment rode high on her cheeks, but she promised herself she would see this through. His large hand stroked up and down along the smooth skin of his shaft, gathering the drop of clear fluid that had beaded on the end and smearing it back along as he stroked down.

The heat in her eyes was enough to burn him. She was so intent on what he was doing that he felt like he could explode at any moment. Her tongue came out to wet her bottom lip, and he felt it on the tip of his dick. He moaned, throwing his head back.

Meredith wondered if he realized how gorgeous he looked standing there in front of her. His feet were planted apart, his stomach muscles tightened in anticipation of what was to come, the veins on his arms sticking out as his hand gripped the hardest part of him. It was like the two of them were in a haze and it made everything that much hotter.

"You've got me so worked up," he whispered, his voice hoarse. "I'm glad I didn't get a chance to get inside you, I'd have embarrassed myself."

That burned her hotter than anything else he could have ever said to her. At this moment in time, she wanted him inside her, but she knew it'd be a mistake. Using her knees to walk over to him, she pressed them together so that the tip of him rubbed against her belly. She wasn't sure how this would feel, but she knew she wanted to feel him. As much of him as she could, regardless of the feelings it brought to the surface.

She leaned down, running her tongue around his nipple, much in the same manner as he'd done with her. The hiss that left his mouth gave her encouragement to do it again, this time using her teeth to nip at the tight skin.

"Goddamn," he mumbled, his hand moving faster along his length.

Remembering what he'd said to her and how hot it'd made her, she stood up on her knees and put her lips to his ear. "Give it to me, Tyler," she whispered, letting her teeth run along his earlobe.

His whole body tightened, and he growled as she felt the heat of his release splatter against her belly. Surprisingly, it didn't disgust her, it didn't make her feel cheap. It made her feel hot, it turned her on again.

Leaning back, she looked up into his eyes and smiled as he heaved deep breaths, trying to regulate himself back to normal.

"For someone who doesn't know what they're doing when it comes to sex, baby, you've rocked my world, and we haven't even gotten to the good stuff yet."

A feeling of accomplishment washed over her. Maybe she wasn't so bad at any of this. Maybe she'd just needed someone to pull it out of her.

"What do you say we go take a shower?" she asked, hopping off the bed, not even bothering to wipe herself off.

He ran a hand over his eyes. "Shower? Sounds good." He seemed a bit out of it, and that was the best gift of all.

Chapter Fourteen

I took back a major part of myself today. The part of myself that had been missing. I let Tyler touch me in ways that I've never let a human being touch me before. Both physical and emotional. It feels like a part of me has healed. That gaping hole that was once in my stomach – causing all those jitters – it's gone. I'm happy and ready. Ready to move on. Ready to find my rapist. I just need to figure out how to tell other people. What if they try to talk me out of it?

"You warm enough?"

His deep voice caused so many feelings in her now. He wasn't just the man who protected her now. He was her lover and it felt so right. The mere fact that she was writing in her journal – in his arms – and trusting him not to be nosey, said an awful lot about how far she had come.

"Sure am," she assured him lazily.

It had started raining, and she told him how much she loved the rain in the country and how it sounded against the tin of his roof. He'd suggested they go out back where he had a covered porch and a swing. He'd given her a pair of his sweats and a sweatshirt, and he'd grabbed a blanket for them to snuggle under. She now lay, cuddled against his lap as he used his toe to swing them back and forth.

"I can't believe you have this back here, I never pictured you as the type."

He shrugged and threw his arm along the back of the swing. "All my life I've strived for normal because I never had it growing up. I always wanted a porch swing growing up, so this was the first thing I did. I've never been out here with anyone else before."

There was the opening she'd been looking for. "You mean never been out here on the swing with anybody else or had anybody else here in general."

"Both, kind of" he clarified for her. "The guys don't really come into my private sanctuary. Liam's helped me with some of the remodeling, but nobody else cares to come here. You see how scared of the cup they are," he grinned.

"I think you should be honest about the cup, at least with me," she huffed.

He made the motion of zipping his lips and throwing away the key. "I'll never tell."

"Is it okay for us to be here for this long? I know you've been doing stuff for the club and I hate to take you away from that," she changed the subject.

"I let Liam know I'd be off the grid for possibly a few days."

"A few days, huh?" The smile that lit up her face caused every masculine part of his body to take notice.

"Well, you never know," he tried to play it off. "I mean I didn't think we'd spend two or three days here screwing like bunnies, but I thought maybe we could spend some time alone together," he rushed to cover up.

"I'm just giving you a hard time," she smacked him in the stomach. "I would love to spend some alone time with you."

This was the part of their relationship that made him nervous. One look in her eyes and he wanted to spill his entire life story, but he'd never been the type to talk a lot about his past. With her though, he knew that it wasn't fair to keep himself hidden away. For the two of them to work, there had to be honesty. He'd never had that in any kind of relationship before except in his club. It was scary.

"Do I make you nervous?" she asked after the long beat of silence had passed between them.

"You scare the fuck out of me," he admitted on a laugh. She watched as he ran his hands through his hair.

"How?"

"You make me want to tell you everything and lay my soul bare. Especially after what you shared with me today, but I'm scared to do that. I don't have a good track record with people at all, and I don't want to send you running for the hills."

His honesty touched her more than anything else could have and at the same time it broke her heart.

"You can tell me whatever you want to, Ty. It doesn't have to be your life story and it doesn't have to be anything you don't want to share with me. Whatever you're comfortable with."

He wanted to laugh at her use of those words. They were the words he was constantly using for her. Maybe they had needed each other; maybe they'd been brought together by a force greater than themselves. For the first time, he believed that it wasn't just a coincidence that he'd been driving by on the night of her attack, maybe it'd been the plan all along. Comfortably, she settled back against his lap, enjoying their quiet time together.

Liam sighed, he really needed Tyler. This protection run had turned FUBAR from the word go. William was breathing down his neck about these damn protection runs. It didn't help that they had been voted on by the club as the first show of solidarity towards Liam. Showing that they were perhaps ready to move in a different direction with another man at the head of the table. If this didn't go well, Liam knew he would never hear the end of it.

"I'm gonna tell you one more time Jagger, get this shit straight," he yelled at the new brother who couldn't seem to find his way out of a paper bag.

He'd been given the opportunity to drive point tonight on this run and he'd gotten them lost, even with a mother-fucking GPS.

"It was right before we left, I swear to you," he argued, hitting the GPS that kept giving them different directions, no matter how many times he set the destination on it.

Losing his patience, Liam grabbed it out of the other man's hands. "Steele, fix this fuckin' thing and get us the fuck out of here. Denise expected me an hour ago, and I'll be damned if I'm sleepin' on the couch because dimwit over here can't work a piece of technology. Not to mention I'm gonna disappoint my son because he's playing a damn football game right now," Liam growled. The tension between him and his father – that they had kept between the two of them for the most part — made his words much rougher than he intended.

Steele walked over and grabbed the GPS, putting the destination in again and laughing when it showed them the correct route. "What the hell were you doin', Jagger?"

"The same fuckin' thing you just did."

"Curse of the skull mug strikes again," Steele advised him. "Told you not to touch that thing."

Blowing out a frustrated breath, Jagger screamed. "No one told me not to touch it."

"Let's just get the hell out of here," Liam said, not able to help the grin that came to his face. Jagger was never going to live this down.

"You hungry?" Tyler asked.

They had been sitting outside for hours. Nighttime had already come pitch black, and with it, much cooler temperatures. November in Kentucky could be a crap shoot. Sometimes it was very cool, sometimes they suffered through an Indian summer. This year, it was already turning cool.

"Yeah, but I'm so warm and comfortable with you right here. I don't wanna get up," she admitted.

Just then his stomach gave a loud growl. They both laughed and she sat up, bringing the blanket with her.

"I guess we better feed you."

The two of them walked into the house, holding hands. He directed them into the kitchen and walked over to the refrigerator. "I don't even know what I have here. Hopefully something halfway decent."

She reached up into the cabinets, trying to find staples. Finally opening a door with food behind it, she spotted some cans of soup. "Do you have cheese and bread? We can have soup and grilled cheese."

That was agreeable to both of them, and they worked alongside each other in a comfortable silence. When it was done, they had a seat at the kitchen table and began eating.

He moaned as he took a bite of the grilled cheese. "This is so good," he praised her.

"Thanks, just like my mom used to make. I loved when I was little and it was almost winter and we'd have grilled cheese and chicken noodle or tomato soup. Those are some of my best memories." That was the only time she ever really felt like she and her mother had something in common with one another. They would sit for hours over their soup, talking until her dad got home, and then the conversation would turn to what he expected her to do when she grew up.

Immediately she felt bad, he didn't have those memories and she could see it in his eyes. Even if hers weren't great, she still had them. He took another large bite and swallowed loudly. "Would it freak you out if I told you I want to make those memories with you?"

She set down her food and grasped his hand. "Not at all. I wanna make those memories with you too."

Chapter Fifteen

"**D**id I miss anything important?"

Liam looked up from where he sat on the garage floor, putting together some parts for a bike he was working on. "I'm so glad you're back, man. Oh my God, it's been crazy since you left."

"I was only gone for a little bit," Tyler laughed, pulling over a chair so that he could have a seat.

"The curse of your damn cup is alive and well. Jagger got us lost, the GPS wouldn't work for him, he's still nursing himself from that fall, and to top it all off he broke the starter on his bike," he held up the parts in his hands.

"How did he do that?"

"Like I need to tell you. Everyone firmly believes it's your curse."

Tyler laughed so hard tears streamed down his face. "This is getting way out of hand. I never thought that cup would cause all this grief. This is great."

"Is it cursed or not?" Liam asked, leveling a glare at the other man.

"Don't try to scare me with that look. You know I don't scare easily. It is whatever you think it is," he said cryptically.

"You're getting on my nerves about this fuckin' curse," Liam mumbled. "Fuck," he screamed as his wrench flew off the part he was trying to fix.

Tyler laughed again. "You should watch that blood pressure, old man. It can sometimes get to ya."

"You're not gonna tell me the truth," he yelled at Tyler's retreating form.

"You already know the truth."

"Cryptic bullshit is gonna be the death of me," Liam mumbled as he took a deep breath and went back to work.

"Denise, you here?" Meredith yelled as she lightly knocked on the front door.

"Upstairs, come on up."

That was unusual, Denise upstairs towards the bedroom this late in the day. Meredith checked her watch to make sure she was right on the time of day. Sure enough, it was a quarter after one.

"You okay?" she asked as she came into the bedroom.

Denise was on the ground in front of the toilet, lying on the cool tile floor. "Something I ate totally did not agree with me. I've been sick since this morning," she moaned.

"What did you eat?" Meredith asked, having a seat on the floor and leaning against the front of the tub.

"We had a cookout at the clubhouse. I really think it could have been the shrimp. As long as I stay horizontal on the cool tile, I'm fine. Enough about me, how were the past couple of days for you?"

The blush that covered her face couldn't be helped. "It was good," she admitted.

"Oh c'mon. I'm lying on the bathroom floor after puking my guts out. Give me just a little bit more than that. Tyler Blackfoot is a hot piece of man meat and you're telling me it was good."

"It was better than good, it was amazing. I can't even describe how great it was."

"Are you feeling better about yourself?" Denise asked carefully. She'd known without Meredith having to mention a lot to her that she was feeling pretty low.

"You know, I am. I feel like I've reclaimed a part of myself. I mean, don't get me wrong, we didn't have sex, but we made such a step forward in our relationship. We talked, we ate, we just hung out. It was, hands down, the nicest time I've ever spent with a man."

Denise nodded in agreement. "You know until I met Liam, I never really knew what a nice time with a man was either. Funny how everyone wants to label these guys as outlaws, but they're nothing but perfect gentlemen to us."

"Funny how that works out, huh?" Meredith laughed.

"It's good to see you laugh." Denise smiled. "I know we weren't exactly close when all of this went down. Actually, I think I kinda hated you for coming into my house and trying to tell me how to run my business."

"I really shouldn't have done that," Meredith cringed, covering her face with her hands.

"No, I think your heart was in the right place, even if you were a bit of a bitch about it."

"You are such a nice person. My heart was all about getting up in your business and getting an anchor spot on the news," she shook her head. "I was so naïve and selfish, and all I could think about was myself. When I wonder why all this stuff has happened to me, I just think about how selfish I was."

"Don't even think that. Yes, you were kind of annoying, but you were trying to better yourself. No one deserves what you went through, Meredith. Nobody."

"Is it bad for me to say, I'm kinda glad it happened the way it did? I mean there's no way I would ever want to be raped, but I'm glad it brought me to the place I'm at now. I've never had a friend like you before, never had someone to hang out with or anything. I was always too busy working and trying to make something of myself to get involved with anybody else in any kind of way. I'm glad it opened up my eyes."

The past few days have been some of the most amazing of my life. I feel like I'm finally healing, like maybe that's what Doc Jones wanted me to do all along. I feel like I can finally breathe and I'm not going to break down at every curveball that's thrown at me. For the first time I feel strong.

Meredith sat her journal down with a sense of accomplishment. The words she'd just written she truly believed. No matter what life threw at her, she would be able to handle it. In the back of her mind, she realized another truth. She was ready to find her rapist. She wasn't sure how, but she would find him.

Tyler came through the door scowling, only to grin as he caught sight of her. "Hey."

She flirted back, "Hey, I have a favor to ask you."

He had a seat beside her and turned so that he faced her, showing that she had his full attention.

"I want to find my rapist."

The words hit him like a ton of bricks. That was his dream too. He had mentioned it a few times to her, but she had blown him off. Now, it looked as if their minds were as connected as their bodies were. "I want to find him too. I've already been looking, to be perfectly honest with you, but there's not a whole lot to go on."

"I have contacts in the community from my days at the news station. There has to be someone who can help. Those days after are such a blur to me, I still don't quite understand what all happened. I had a lot of people telling me things about the clubs around here. Someone knows who this guy is. Someone paid him to do it, and they did it to send me a message. I want to know why. What was I on to or what did I uncover?"

This made him uneasy. What if she got close to it again? What would they do to her this time? Now the stakes were so much higher. "I don't know if I like this," he admitted.

"What do you think I was on to?"

"I have no idea, we weren't exactly talkin' buddies back then if you remember," he grinned.

"I wanted to be. I thought you were so hot."

It was unlike her to gush, but he liked it. Her giddiness was cute. "I thought you were pretty hot yourself. Why don't you get all your stuff out of storage and we can comb through it. Maybe fresh eyes and your time away from it will give us an idea."

He had a good point and she was agreeable to it. "Will you take me over there tomorrow to get the stuff? I don't wanna go by myself."

"I don't want you going over there by yourself either. I have a run tomorrow, so I'll let you know when I'm available."

"Oh, so I need to pencil myself in?" she played along with him.

"You know me, I'm busy, but I'll do my best to make time for you."

This playful side of him was new and she loved it. There were numerous facets to this man who she previously had thought of as being only one dimensional. It showed her again just how much she'd had her eyes closed to the world around her before. Her eyes were definitely open now, and she was going to make sure she never missed anything again.

Chapter Sixteen

"Where is the semi?"

Liam had the exact same question. They had been sitting in the parking lot of a local clothing manufacturer for over an hour. Word had it that the manufacturer was in deep with the Mexican Cartel and within some of the shipments of clothing lay weapons that were needed to win the drug war. Since Heaven Hill had signed on to help, they were expected to make sure the semis got to the state line where another MC picked up the run.

"This guy was supposed to come here, drop off his trailer, pick up another, and be gone, right?" Liam verified with Jagger. "You didn't fuck this one up, right?"

His nerves were on a string. His eyes met William's and he could see the triumph there. This wasn't working out and William knew it. Almost like the fucker had planned it. Their relationship was strained, at best, these days. It made Liam and his guys look weak.

"I didn't. I think I've finally gotten over the curse of the cup. I've gone a full fifteen hours with nothing bad happening to me," he knocked on his head for effect. "This run was written down and verified by Tyler."

"I thought so," Tyler agreed, putting a cigar in his mouth and lighting it. "I've talked to this motherfucker like three times. He knew what time to be here. Something must have happened."

"Call one of the girls," William advised. "Make sure he didn't get picked up or there wasn't an accident. They should be manning that scanner."

Turning away from the rest of the group so that he would be able to hear well, Tyler made the call. When the call was picked up and he heard Meredith's voice, he was surprised.

"Hey where's Denise?" he asked quietly. He didn't want to alert Liam that she wasn't at her usual spot running the scanner for them.

"Still sick, she's either in bed or running to the bathroom. I seriously need to get her to the ER, but she insisted that you guys needed help with this. I manned the scanner when I was at the news station, so this has been kind of fun. I've written stuff down that sounds interesting to me, but I really don't know what I'm listening for," she explained.

He blew out a breath of smoke and sighed. "Okay, first we'll get this run over with and then we'll deal with Denise."

"Are you smoking?" she broke in. "I've smelled it and tasted it on you, but I've never seen you do it."

"Yeah, cigars, made with a friend's tobacco. They aren't something you can buy in a store. I like mine sweet."

That explained why he always tasted so sweet when she kissed him.

"I need info on a truck driver, he should have been driving a semi headed toward the warehouse we're at. Look at the GPS signal on the computer connected to the scanner. You should be able to see right where we are. I don't know where he was coming from, but he should have had a trailer attached."

She scrolled through the notes she'd made, things that interested her. She found one where she'd noted a license plate number and the fact that it was a semi.

"Looks like your boy did get picked up. I made a note of a semi with an Alabama license plate. Rooster pulled him over about an hour ago, and they impounded the semi. Driver was taken to jail. Charges didn't come over the scanner though. At least, I didn't write them down so he may not have gone before the judge yet."

"Fuckin' Rooster. Alright, I'll see you in a bit then," he slammed the phone closed and wanted to scream. He hated when things didn't go as planned.

"Rooster got our boy."

There was a groan that rumbled through the group. "Damn it," Liam yelled. "Guess we're headin' back to the house."

Tyler put his hand on Liam's shoulder, holding him back from the group. "Meredith said Denise is still sick and she's contemplating taking her to the ER."

"I told that woman that I wouldn't leave if she was still sick, and she told me she was fine. She even smiled when I left. I had no idea she was still feeling bad," his glare would have melted other men.

"Now don't go in there all pissed off at her. If she's still puking, that's two days straight. She probably feels like shit."

"Point made. How do we convince her to get her ass to the ER?"

"We'll figure it out, let's get the hell outta here."

"Did you tell Liam that I'm still sick?"

Meredith couldn't help but grin. "So what if I did?"

"I'll kill you," Denise threatened from her place on the bed.

"When and how? You can't get up for more than a few minutes and when you do, you're head is hanging over the toilet. Nice try. Besides, I told Tyler, not Liam."

"Might as well have, the two of them share a brain for the most part."

Going over to the dresser, Meredith opened the drawers and grabbed a clean pair of sweatpants and a clean t-shirt. "C'mon, let's get you dressed. We'll get you to the hospital when Tyler and Liam get here."

It was on the tip of Denise's tongue to tell her to fuck off, but at the last moment her stomach lurched again. Maybe Meredith was right, something about this was off. She couldn't deny how weak she felt. "Okay, I think I'm gonna need your help."

By the time the roar of motorcycles could be heard coming up the drive, Meredith had Denise down the stairs and sitting on the couch. A trash can sat in front of her, one that she'd already had to use a few times. Though nothing other than stomach acid came up anymore.

Meredith ran to the front door, waving at Tyler and Liam. They cut off their motorcycles and ran towards the front porch.

"How is she?" Liam asked, his fear written on his face.

"Still sick. I convinced her to go to the doctor. She's sitting on the couch dressed. I really don't think she has the energy to walk out here to your truck."

"Where are my kids?" he asked as he took off his chaps and road gear to try and calm his nerves. When he had brought Denise into the fold of this family, he had brought along her twin teenage children. Everyone had taken to them as if they had been in the family since the beginning.

"Roni's, Denise had already sent them over when I got here. She did the same thing to them as she did to you – sent them off with a smile."

"Damn her," he growled, stowing his stuff in his saddle bags.

She watched as he took the stairs of the porch two at a time and thundered through the front door.

"Hey," Meredith smiled at Tyler.

"Hey yourself. Thanks for convincing her to go to the doctor. When I told him she was still sick, it looked like he was about ready to ring her neck."

"Yeah well so was I. While they're gone, do you think we can make that time to go get that stuff out of storage?" she asked.

"Should be alright," he shrugged. "The run for tonight was called off since our driver got arrested. Some of the guys are going to see what they can find out about that. I came with him to make sure Denise is alright. Since he's taking her to the ER, I really don't have anything else to do. Consider the time made," he teased.

She reached out, pinching him on the arm. "Thanks so much, I'm glad I rank that high."

The teasing stopped as Liam came out of the front door, carrying Denise in his arms. He tossed the keys at Tyler. "Open the door and let the seat down so she doesn't have to sit straight up."

The other man caught them with one hand and beat feet over to where the truck was parked. As Liam held Denise close, running a hand over her forehead, Tyler worked quickly to do as instructed. When he was finally done, he stood back to allow Liam to place her inside the truck.

"I brought a blanket, just in case," Meredith reached in, putting it around her friend, tucking her in as she would a child. "Snug as a bug in a rug," she whispered, causing a weak smile to spread across Denise's face.

"Let us know how things go," Tyler said as he stood with Meredith, an arm around her shoulders.

"Will do, we'll see y'all in a bit."

"Whatever you do, when they make you wait, don't cause a scene," Meredith warned Liam.

"I know, I'll do my best, but I can't promise shit."

That was the best she could ask for. As the truck drove down the drive, the couple stood watching the fading brake lights.

"While we wait for them, let's go check out that storage unit," Tyler said, grabbing her hand and pulling her to the bike with him.

"I missed you," she admitted, reaching up on tiptoes to kiss him.

"Good to know, I'll take that greeting anytime you wanna give it. Let's get out of here and find out what we all missed the first time around."

A feeling settled in her stomach, heavy enough that it felt like it was holding her down. She knew the answers to her questions lay there, but she still wasn't sure if she wanted those answers or not.

Chapter Seventeen

"What do you want from out of here?" Tyler asked, gazing at the sheer volume of stuff that was wedged inside the storage unit.

She thought for a moment. "Anything marked research. I know there are a couple of boxes. I need the laptop and the two computers as well as the contents of my desk."

"Well we didn't plan this out too well, did we?" he laughed, looking at his bike. "Let me call Jagger and have him bring my truck."

"You have a truck?" This was news to her.

"And a car. I'm mysterious," he wiggled his eyebrows up and down.

There were so many things she didn't know about this man, and the more she found out, the more she wanted to know. "What kind of truck and car do you have?"

"Your normal boys' toys," he shrugged.

"Jagger, I need you to bring my truck to the storage unit that Meredith's stuff is in. If you can manage it, try not to break anything and try not to wreck it." Without even saying goodbye, he hung up.

"Why are y'all so mean to him?"

"He's new, we're always mean to the new ones. I guess I could be a little bit nicer to him since he did get my curse, huh?" he teased, a bright smile on his face.

Not rising to the bait, she came over to stand in front of him. "Whatever you say, Mr. Blackfoot. Do you want to go ahead and start getting some of this stuff out, or do you want to just wait on him?"

He looked around, and seeing no one else but them, he stepped closer to her. At one time, being this close to him would have made her nervous, but now she was used to it, actually ached to be this close to him.

"I think we can just wait on him."

His large hands went to her hair and tangled there, tilting her head just the way he wanted before his lips claimed hers.

She moaned when his mouth captured hers. Almost immediately she let him take over, direct her in how he wanted to take her mouth. His tongue stroked the roof roughly, taking more than she dared let him take before. Unable to prevent it, her hands went around his body, holding him closer to her. They pressed together in the darkness of the storage lot, a light a few feet away the only thing keeping them out of complete darkness. Letting his hands slide down from her hair, he ran them softly to her neck, needing to feel skin against skin.

Pulling her lips from his, she smeared her lips down his neck, stopping to suck at the pulse point in the middle. His heart beat wildly under the smoothness of her lips. It made her feel empowered, to make his heart beat this fast.

"You burn me up," he admitted as she used her teeth to lightly nip at that same point on his neck.

She stepped back, looking up into his eyes. "I'm glad. You burn me up too, it's only fair."

He ran his hands down her back and gripped her around the waist, backing up against the side of the building. Making her feel like she weighed little more than a feather, he easily lifted her up and pressed her there with the weight of his body. Unconsciously, she wrapped her legs around his waist.

"If this doesn't become good with you, you let me know," he whispered fiercely to her.

The fact that he always worried about her pissed her off and warmed her heart all at the same time. While she wished he didn't have to worry about anything, she was so glad that he did. "Understood."

Pushing her up higher against the building put her nipple even with his mouth. She grabbed his hair as his tongue soothed the hardness through the layers of her shirt and bra. It was madness, she'd never been in this situation before. All she knew was having him go all alpha male on her was the hottest thing she'd ever seen in her life. His large hands grasped the globes of her ass as he squeezed them, pressing her nipple deeper into his mouth.

Her feet dug into his lower back as he ate at her, wanting him closer. She wanted to feel some part of his skin that didn't have clothing on it, but he'd been dressed for battle. Long sleeves covered his arms, leathers covered his legs.

"I wanna feel you," she moaned in frustration.

Bringing his hands from her ass he moved them around to the front of her body, caressing her stomach before moving them further up. Goosebumps broke out on her flesh as she felt his fingers run up her naked skin. She loved the feel of his hands against her. It was becoming her favorite feeling in the world.

"Not enough," she complained.

This had quickly gotten out of hand, he realized. In the background, he could hear the roar of what he knew was his truck. He had to stop this before Jagger caught them in an even more compromising position. Setting her down, he pulled her shirt so that it covered her bare stomach and tried to push her hair back into place. He tried to fix the things he could.

What he couldn't fix was the wild look in her eyes, the swollen lips that even now begged for his kiss, the wet spot on the front of her t-shirt, the out of control cadence of her breathing.

"Bad place to start that, huh?" he tried to lighten the mood.

"Can we finish this later?" she asked as she saw Jagger pull up behind Tyler's shoulder. "Jagger's here."

"Absolutely," he promised. "Put this on," he instructed her.

He took off his cut and the long sleeved shirt he had on. Underneath the long sleeved shirt, he wore a tank top. Throwing the shirt towards her, he put his cut back on and turned to face Jagger. He really didn't want his brother seeing the wet spot on her shirt. Walking over, he intercepted him to give her time to put the shirt on over her we one.

"Thanks for coming. Did you have any issues getting' out here?"

"Nope," Jagger smiled confidently. "Like I told you, I think I've broken the curse."

Tyler couldn't help but grin. "Whatever you say."

He instructed Jagger on what they needed to get out of the storage unit, not letting Meredith pick up or move anything. She grumbled as she sat on the sidelines watching them do all the work. Every now and again she would get a text from Denise or Liam telling her that they were giving Denise fluids and then running some tests on her. One text she got made her stomach clench.

"They're keeping Denise overnight," she told the other two.

"Do they know what's wrong with her?" Tyler asked, concern etched on his face.

In her heart, Meredith thought she knew what was wrong with her friend. Denise had avoided all questions that she had asked about a diagnosis. She'd only said she'd talk to her face-to-face in the morning.

"Not yet. I need to talk to you later though."

He looked at her, not sure what she wanted to talk to him about and why it seemed to have something to do with his friends. "When we get to the clubhouse, I'll be sure and make time for you."

"Thanks," she laughed. "I'm glad I'm important enough for you to make time for."

A few hours later, they'd loaded everything into the truck, and Tyler directed Jagger on where to take it and unload it.

"Do you really think the answer to why and who attacked me is in that stuff?" she asked him as they watched Jagger drive away.

"I'm not sure, but I truly think that there may be a good clue there. What happened to you wasn't some random act of violence. It wasn't like someone came upon you and just decided to violate you. It was an attack, it was personal, and it was planned. Now if that had anything to do with me, I sure as hell want to know about it. I wanna make things right if it's because of this club, and I will take it out of the man's hide. Don't doubt that."

The look on his face told her how serious he was. She didn't doubt him at all, and the murderous glint in his eyes spoke of just how serious he was.

Chapter Eighteen

Meredith ran her hands through her hair as she surveyed the amount of stuff they'd stacked into an empty room at the clubhouse. It was a lot more than she had originally anticipated. To say she didn't know where to start would be a huge understatement.

"This is the last of it," Tyler said as he brought in a drawer that went in her desk. "More than you thought?" he asked as he noticed the panicked look on her face.

"Yeah, is it that obvious?" she bit her thumbnail as she asked that question.

"You look a little overwhelmed."

He had a seat on one of the boxes and pulled her over to him so that she stood in between his legs. "Is that all that's goin' on here? What did you want to talk to me about earlier?"

She sighed as she had a seat on his leg and wrapped her arms around his neck. For a moment, she buried her face in his neck. He became alarmed when he felt wetness there.

"Hey, hey," he pulled her away and cupped her cheeks. "What's really going on?" he used his thumbs to wipe at the tears streaming down her face. She gulped in breaths of air trying to calm herself down. "What the hell's got you so upset?"

"I think Denise is pregnant," she whispered.

He was confused. What did this have to do with her? "You're gonna have to explain what's goin' through your head because, baby, I definitely am not a mind reader today."

"I'm a horrible, horrible person because I'm jealous."

That threw him. They hadn't even had sex, much less talked about kids, but that statement made him sit up straighter. "Why are you jealous?"

"I want kids someday, but what if because of what happened to me I can't ever bring myself to get there."

"What do you mean?"

She hated this. There was not one part of her that wanted to voice this fear she had to Tyler. Not one part. "What if I can never have sex again?"

He laughed. Straight up belly laughed. "That's what you're worried about? Haven't you been in my arms the last couple of nights? Haven't you thought about having sex with me? Weren't there a few times that we had to stop each other? You will overcome this fear. You're too passionate not to. I'm not pressuring you am I?" He was horrified at the thought. That was the last thing he wanted to do.

"No, not at all. You've been more than patient with me. But what if I can't ever get past it? I want kids, you may want kids."

His heart swelled. She was talking about a future involving the both of them, not two separate beings. "We could always adopt. You forget I'm an orphan."

She slapped her hand over her mouth. She *had* forgotten. This man who offered her so much love and affection had started out in life with none given to him. "I'm so sorry Tyler."

"Don't be. I didn't tell you that to make you feel sorry for me. I'm just giving you other options. Can I share something with you?"

Meredith wanted to know everything that this man wanted to tell her. There was not one part of him that she didn't want to know. "Please, share everything with me."

"For the first two months of my life, I didn't have a name. My name was John Doe. My first birth certificate actually says John Doe. It wasn't until an older Native American couple took me in as foster parents that I got a name. They gave me their family last name. I have no idea who either of my real parents are. But I came into this world as a John Doe."

That hurt her so much. How could someone do that to a child? How could someone nurture that child in their belly for nine months and then leave him alone to face the world? "How come you didn't stay with them?"

"They couldn't afford me. They already had the maximum amount of children they could afford. From what I hear, they tried hard and I was with them for a long time. My first memories of childhood are with that couple. That house I took you to? It was theirs. I bought it when they died a few years ago. That's why I love it so much."

She grappled with all the information he had given her. The strong man who hardly ever revealed anything about himself had dropped two bombs on her in a short amount of time. "Thank you for sharing this with me."

"I wouldn't have done it if I didn't want to. What I'm trying to say about all this though is that there are options. I'm not leaving you no matter what you can or can't do. So if you can never get there, I'll be fine. I'm committed to you and I think you're committed to me."

"I am."

"Have you talked to Doc Jones about this?"

"I have. That's where she came up with the idea of masturbation to try and get me there. I don't know why I'm freaking out about this so much. Life is going to move on whether I'm ready or not."

He caressed her neck and placed a soft kiss on her temple. "That's right, it is going to and none of us know where it's going, Meredith. The only thing we can do is hang on and make the best decisions for us. What say we just live and see where it takes us? We have no plans. We're just two people trying to make the best of situations that were given to us. As long as we live, nothing else can be asked of us."

She took a moment to think about what he had just said. He was right. She was getting all worked up again over things that were so far out of her control they might as well be in another universe. Calmed down, she took a deep breath. "You're right, as always."

"What was that? I think I heard you say I was right?"

She giggled and pushed his shoulder. "You know that you're wise, I don't need to stroke your ego anymore."

Wanting to put a little bit of playfulness into what had become a very serious discussion, he winked. "I got something else you can stroke."

She pushed herself off his knee. "Tyler Blackfoot! You behave."

"You're the one who asked if we could continue our little interlude later, but that's okay, I can take a rain check if you can."

She flounced out of the room, slinging her hair back as she got to the door. Turning, she stared at him over her shoulder and gave him a look before crooking her finger at him. "I don't think I can."

For a six foot three inch man, he was extremely agile and had made his way to her in just a few steps. Picking her up, he threw her over his shoulder and made his way to his dorm room.

"I knew you couldn't resist me," he teased her as he shut the door. "I'm just way too sexy."

Chapter Nineteen

"I'm so glad you're here," Denise welcomed Meredith into the hospital room she still occupied.

Meredith waved, trying to be quiet as she saw Liam curled up in the corner on a pulled out cot. "Should I come back later?" she whispered, pointing at Liam.

"Nah, I'm up," he sat up, yawning as he ran his hands over his eyes. "Did Tyler bring you?"

"Yeah, he's downstairs grabbing some coffee. He told me to let you know if you were awake, you could come join. I think he was gonna go get some breakfast at Donna's."

"Oh, I am all over that. This hospital food sucks donkey balls. You don't mind do you?" he asked her as he sat up, straightening his clothes out.

"Sure don't."

"You'll be good?" Liam asked, turning to face Denise.

"I'll be fine. I told you that you could go home last night. Remember?"

Meredith watched as they argued good-naturedly.

"I am not leaving you up here in this place by yourself. Don't even ask me to do that again. I thought we settled that."

"We did," she grumbled.

He leaned down and kissed her forehead. "I have my cell if you need me."

Denise did her best not to roll her eyes. "Meredith is here. I am going to be fine. Now go!"

The two women watched as he exited the room. When the door shut, Denise growled. "He is driving me absolutely insane."

Meredith couldn't help but laugh. "He loves you, he's just worried."

"I know, I know. My hormones are just out of control."

They lapsed into a comfortable silence. "So how far along are you?" Meredith asked quietly.

"Five weeks. Are you mad? Because that's the last thing I want." Denise scrunched up her nose and twisted her fingers together.

"Not at all. Please don't ever think I was mad at *you*. It was myself I was mad at, and after talking to Tyler, I realize how stupid I was being. I am so *happy* for you and Liam."

"You don't know how happy I am to hear that. You've become my best friend, and I didn't want to hurt you in any way. That day we talked about this, I never realized how hurt your feelings would be, and I realized how insensitive I was being."

Meredith stopped her as she held a hand up. "No, I was being insensitive. Just because something awful happened to me doesn't give me the right to be a bitch to all others around me. I was being selfish and I'm sorry. I am genuinely so happy for you two. What's going on with you being in here though? Is everything okay?"

A huge weight felt like it had been lifted off of the friends, they were no longer tiptoeing around one another. Meredith scooted her chair all the way up to the bed so that they could converse without having so much distance.

"I had horrible morning sickness with the twins, but I figured it was just because there were two of them. Apparently, I'm one of the lucky women who just has a hard time with morning sickness. They did an ultrasound yesterday, and there is only one baby and I think I'm sicker now than I ever was with twins."

Meredith grimaced. "I'm so sorry. Can they do anything for you?"

"They have me on some anti-nausea medication and they are pumping fluids into me because I was dehydrated. There's a pill I can take that might help, but it's not always the case with every pregnant woman. We'll just have to see I guess. They were just worried about me being so dehydrated. Thank you for making me come to the hospital when you did by the way."

"That's what friends are for. I knew you looked bad and I knew you would never tell someone that you needed to. I just made an executive decision."

They gossiped for a little while before Denise asked about her getting her stuff out of storage. "How did that go?"

"Alright I guess. I haven't had a chance to go through it all. I was going to last night, but I got busy," she muttered, her cheeks flushing a bright red.

"Got busy doing what? Or should I say who?"

"It wasn't exactly like that, but I can say we're moving closer to a normal relationship."

Denise smiled brightly. "Do you know how thrilled I am to hear that? I think most women that even see Tyler Blackfoot fall just a little bit in love with him. You are one lucky woman."

Meredith giggled. "We both are really. Our men are hot."

"That they are," Denise agreed, laughing along as the door opened and the two men appeared.

"It's never good when we walk in and they're both giggling." Liam said, walking over to the cot and having a seat. He patted his belly and sighed deeply.

"Did you eat?" Denise asked, completely ignoring his statement.

"I did and it was glorious. Bacon, eggs, sausage, and home fries. Damn, that woman can cook."

"My mouth just watered, but I know if I could smell it, I would be back in the bathroom upchucking," Denise groused.

"Congrats by the way," Tyler said from the doorway.

"Thank you," she beamed. "I think we're pretty excited."

Liam nodded his head in agreement as he lay back down on the cot.

"How much longer are you in here for?" Meredith asked as she stood and went to stand by Tyler.

It was so natural for her to step in front of him and have his arms come around her waist. He bent so that his head rested on her shoulder, his hair tangling with hers.

Denise couldn't help but notice the change in Meredith as she leaned back into Tyler's arms. It brought a smile to her face. "A couple days probably. They want to try to get the morning sickness under control. I need to be able to eat.'"

Meredith nodded. "Well, we're gonna go, but I'll be back. Is there anything you need? Do you want me to bring the kids next time I come?"

Tyler had things to do over the next couple of days, so that would mean a trip by herself. This was a huge step, that she was even considering it. The anxiety it caused was minimal, and she breathed deeply.

"If you feel like it, I'd love to see them. I do need some more clothes if you wouldn't mind."

"I don't. I'll be back either later tonight or early tomorrow. Take it easy," she told her friend as she leaned down on the bed and gave her a hug.

"I am so happy for you, don't doubt that," she whispered before leaning back up.

"You don't know how much that means to me."

Chapter Twenty

"Jagger, do you think you could come help me?" Meredith yelled from the room that housed her storage materials. Tyler had set a box just a fingertip too high for her to get, and he'd left to go do a run for the club.

She had been going through everything with a fine tooth comb, only stopping to take clothes and the kids to Denise. When the trip had gone off with only a few minor speed bumps, it had reiterated to her that this was the right thing to do. She still had yet to find anything that pointed to her attacker.

"Yeah," Jagger said coming into the room. "What can I do for ya?"

"I need that box up there, Tyler put it a little too high for me to get to it," she pointed to the box in question. "Be careful," she cautioned.

"The curse is over," he pointed out as he grabbed it over his head.

In the blink of an eye, he lost his grip and it fell, busting open. "Fuck," he mumbled.

"Curse is over, huh?" she couldn't help the grin that broke across her face.

"I thought so anyway," he grumbled, bending over to help her pick the stuff up. "Looks like you got some mail here you never opened."

He held a manila envelope out to her and she took it, noting the weight of it. It was very heavy. "Thanks, I don't think I've ever seen this before."

Jagger shrugged, leaving her alone with it. It had her old address on it, along with the correct postage it would need to be sent to her. It was postmarked from Bowling Green on the day that she had been attacked. For some reason her hands shook as she ripped open the top of the envelope. It seemed like whatever this held was important. Like it held the answers to the questions that she had. Turning it over, she poured out the contents and gasped.

Pictures. Hundreds of pictures, all containing females connected to the club. There were numerous pictures of her, Denise, Roni, Mandy, and even Lauren. They all seemed to be taken at different places, like they had been followed. Other pictures contained male members of the club. Quickly she grabbed the envelope again, but it contained no return address. A feeling washed over her, this couldn't have been the only thing that had come for her. Running out of the room, she caught Jagger behind the bar, singing along to a song on the radio. Any other day she would have complemented him on his voice – today though she had other things to speak to him about.

"Has any of my mail been forwarded here?" Her mail had been the last thing on her mind for months. Since she'd broken her lease, she really had no bills save her car and car insurance. She'd never been one to have credit cards, and her school had been taken care of. There really wasn't any reason that she'd need any of her mail. Now though, she had a feeling she'd missed something very important.

"I'm not sure, you want me to look?" he asked, going into the room where most of the paperwork was kept.

"Yes. I need to know if there are any more envelopes." The panicked feeling overtook her, made her stomach cramp.

He looked through some stuff and didn't see anything, but then an idea struck him. "Maybe it's at the shop," meaning *Walker's Wheels* where many of the club members worked during the day.

"Can you call and ask?"

Jagger made a quick phone call and then nodded at her. "Yeah, according to the bookkeeper, Janice, you have four more envelopes there. No one wanted to bother you with it, so she's just been keeping them there for you."

Her stomach churned. She needed to know what was in those envelopes, but she was scared to find out at the same time. "I need those envelopes. When should Tyler be back?"

Jagger checked his watch. "Not for a couple more hours at least. They were going almost to Louisville and back."

"Then you have to take me."

"I can't take you on the back of my bike, it would be disrespectful," he stammered, not wanting to do anything else to piss off the big man that had claimed her for his.

"Not if I'm asking you to," she argued.

"Even more so *because* you're asking me to. Tyler will not be happy."

"He's not here and he won't know," she pleaded.

"Oh he'll know," he mumbled, scrubbing a hand over his face.

"Look," she ran her hands through her hair in distress. "I wouldn't ask you unless it was very important. I would take my own car, but it's in storage and I haven't driven it in months. I would take Tyler's truck, but he's never shown me anything besides a damn bike. I am asking for your help and I'm telling you if you don't take me…I'm taking somebody's bike on my own."

Jagger gasped. "You wouldn't. You'll kill yourself. You have no damn idea how to drive a bike."

She reached around him, grabbing the keys he kept hanging on his pocket. "You take me or I take myself."

"You are just bound and determined to get my ass handed to me by Tyler, aren't you? Fine," he sighed. "Let's go."

Riding on the back of someone else's motorcycle was an eye-opening experience for Meredith. She didn't feel nearly as safe with Jagger, and it was weird being that close to someone besides Tyler. It felt awkward when she held on tighter to go through a curve. As they pulled up to *Walker's Wheels*, she saw William talking on his cell phone. Without a doubt, she knew he was probably reporting to Tyler what he was seeing. Jagger cut off the motor and waited for her to get off before he did the same.

"You're treading on some thin ice," William told Jagger as he walked up to the two of them.

"You ain't tellin' me nothin' I don't already know. My neck is already twitchy."

"Should be your scalp," one of the guys called out, laughing along with the rest of them.

Meredith rolled her eyes. She didn't like jokes about Tyler's ethnicity, and at this point in time she really had no patience. "While you all sit out here and joke about whose dick's bigger, I really need to see my mail."

"C'mon in, honey," a female voice called out from behind her.

She turned around and noticed an older woman stood in the doorway to the office. "I'm Janice. I do the books here and I've been holding that mail for you. Tyler thought you might want it sooner or later. I told him he should just open for you, but he didn't want to invade your privacy."

There it was again, him always knowing and doing what was best for her. She wanted him here with her so badly. Whatever this was, she had a feeling it wasn't going to be good. Janice handed her the manila envelopes, and she counted them, four in total, weighing them each with her hands.

Jagger came in the office. "Why don't you wait for Tyler to get here before you open those? He just called and said he's fifteen minutes away and I should wait here to have my ass handed to me."

Meredith winced. "Sorry," she told him. "I'll talk to him and explain."

"Don't you dare say a word. That's embarrassing. I knew I shouldn't have done it and I did it anyway because I can't seem to say no to you. You remind me too much of my sister."

That was the first time he'd mentioned family, and she really wanted to know more about this new brother who had become entwined in her life but knew now wasn't the time to question him.

She heard Tyler's bike roar into the lot, and her heart sped up. It was mere seconds before he made his way into the office and dragged Jagger out by his cut. "I'm gonna have a word with you," he told Jagger and then pinned his dark gaze on Meredith. "And then I'm gonna have a motherfucking word with you. Don't go anywhere."

Feeling very much like a reprimanded child, she had a seat, envelopes in her lap. Maybe when she was finally able to tell him what exactly was going on, he would calm down. Until then, she focused on regulating her breathing and not hyperventilating. She'd never made him mad before, and she didn't like this feeling at all.

Chapter Twenty-One

Jagger had to admit he was nervous. Standing in front of Tyler, knowing that you'd pissed him the fuck off was not the best feeling in the world.

"You know this is extremely disrespectful, my brother," Tyler started, pacing the room like a caged wolf.

"I know," Jagger swallowed hard. There was no sense in trying to make excuses for what he had done. None of them would matter. Now was the time to take his punishment like a member of this club.

The big man stalked up to him, and he could feel the anger rolling off of him in waves. "I'm holding myself back from beatin' you to a bloody pulp because I know you were just trying to do something nice for the woman I care about. For that I'm going to give you fair warning. You do it again and I will kick your ass from here to next Sunday."

The breath Jagger had been holding came out in a rush. He visibly relaxed. It was then that Tyler grabbed him by the sides of his cut and shoved him against the wall.

"Anyone asks and I gave you motherfuckin' hell. Do not—and I repeat—do not mistake my kindness for weakness. I won't offer it again." The tone of his voice let

Jagger know that he was being completely honest with this statement.

"Understood."

Tyler dropped him from where he'd held him and stepped away, taking a deep breath. Before he exited the room, he literally put his own back against the wall and took a few slow inhales and exhales.

"She really didn't mean anything by it," Jagger offered softly.

"I know, and she's never been around this lifestyle before. That's why I'm tryin' to calm my out of control nerves and anger. She doesn't deserve it, but she needs to know it pissed me the fuck off knowing she was on the back of your goddamn bike."

Meredith sat in the office with Janice, her nerves on edge. The only sound was the tapping of her foot against the floor and the low hum of the space heater they used there.

"He won't hurt ya honey," Janice tried to calm the nerves of the other woman.

"I've never seen him this pissed off before. Much less been the one who did it," Meredith explained sticking her thumbnail between her teeth.

Just as Janice was about to say something else to her, Tyler opened the door and stuck his head inside. He pointed at Meredith. "You, come here now," he crooked his finger at her.

His high-handedness really pissed her off, but she figured it wouldn't be wise to say that to him right at the moment. *Maybe that's a conversation for another time*, she thought. Silent, she followed him through the door out to the parking lot, where his bike was.

"Get on," he instructed her. Obviously, they were going for a ride.

Reprimanded, she put the manila envelopes into one of the saddle bags, put her helmet on, and reluctantly got on the back of the bike.

It didn't escape Tyler's attention that through the ride she didn't hold his waist as tight as she normally did and she sure as hell didn't sit as close. He hated that she knew his anger, but he also knew he had a right to it.

She was surprised when they pulled up in front of his house. This couldn't be good, he wanted to be alone. He stopped the bike, and they both sat there in the silence after he shut it off. Neither one of them made a move. Gradually, she moved her hands to his back and ran them up the muscles there, her touch so soft he probably could barely feel her.

"I don't want to be angry with you, but we have to talk about this. You have to understand some rules if we're goin' to keep doin' this," he explained. His voice was full of gravel, like he didn't want to have to tell her the things he knew he needed to. It was obvious he didn't think he should have to.

"I know and I'll take my punishment." Her words surprised her, but she knew they were the truth. The understanding that they had come to in their relationship was that compromise and trust went both ways. He had done so much for her, it was time for her to do something for him.

Squaring his shoulders, he got off the bike and then held out his hand to help her off the back of it. Before walking inside, she reached into the saddlebags and grabbed out her important documents. "When we're done with whatever this is going to be, I really do need to speak with you about this."

He brought his hand up to her cheek and cupped it slightly. "We will," he promised.

They walked inside the house, and he led her to the bedroom that she loved so much, that held such good memories for her. Maybe he wanted to put her at ease because of the memories they shared there. He had a seat on the bed and spread his long legs out in front of him.

"You can't be on the back of another man's bike," his voice turned hard. "That's completely disrespectful to me. If I ever catch you on the back of a man's bike besides Liam, who I trust with my life, I won't be happy. In fact I may just kill the motherfucker right there. Hearing about you on the back of Jagger's bike pissed me the fuck off. That seat, when you ride bitch, at least for me is my woman's seat. I thought you understood that."

In reality she hadn't. She hadn't grown up a part of this culture. She knew that it was important, but she didn't realize it was *that* important.

He continued. "You need a ride, I'll give you one. You need a ride when I'm not around, you take my truck, my car, you ask Denise or another woman for a ride. You don't get on the back of another man's bike. Are we clear?"

She ground her back teeth.

"I can tell you want to lay into me, so I'm giving you permission right here, right now. Tell me what you're thinkin'. It's good to see some fire back in your eyes. Fight me on this, I'm begging you."

She felt a spark of how she used to be. The bulldog who didn't let go of the story. "First of all, I didn't know what truck or car was yours. You never told me. I didn't know where your keys were. Again, you never told me. Besides they're yours, not mine."

"What's mine is yours. I thought we'd covered that."

"No, we haven't. You may *think* I know what we're doing here, but I really have no damn clue. Like you told me the other day, I'm not a mind reader. You've got to *tell* me things."

Tyler didn't like his words thrown back in his face. "Don't turn this around on me."

"I'm not. I'm just explaining to you that I felt like I had no choice. You did not provide me with the tools I needed to get my job done. I made the best decision that I knew in order to get that job done."

"What job?" he was confused now.

"I'm trying to figure out who the fuck raped me. You failed to mention I had mail at the shop. Why did you do that?"

He didn't like being questioned, especially by her and especially when she reverted to reporter mode. Frustrated he ran a hand through his hair. "Because you weren't ready for it."

"How dare you tell me what I'm ready for!"

"Go ahead baby, get pissed. The fact of the matter is, before today you've never really *been* angry. Not really. You're fuming right now. You've been walking around in a cloud. You're actually showing some emotion here, and if you have to get mad at me to do it, then do it."

That even pissed her off. "You don't get to make decisions for me, Tyler Blackfoot."

"Someone has to," the arrogant smile that spread across his face did exactly what he wanted it to. It pushed her past all the emotions she'd been holding inside. It broke through the careful wall she had erected around herself that only allowed the sadness to come through.

With a growl, she launched herself at Tyler, fists flying as she tore into him.

Chapter Twenty-Two

He sat there on the bed, taking the blows that she directed towards his body. She was pissed and they hurt, but he would take whatever she could dish out.

"Stop making decisions for me, I am my own person and I can make my own decisions," she cried out, pushing him back on the bed where he landed with a thump.

"Then start making them," he goaded her.

She realized he was right. She hadn't made any kind of decision really without talking it over with someone since her attack. Doc Jones, him, Denise. Someone always had to be a sounding board before she made her decision or plan of attack. It stopped tonight, it stopped right now.

"What are you doing?" he asked as he caught the glint of defiance in her eyes.

"Making my own decision," she thrust the words out at him.

He watched as she kicked off her shoes and then reached down to the button of her jeans. Within moments she'd unbuttoned them and stripped herself of the heavy material, along with her underwear. The long sleeve shirt she wore was next, along with her bra.

"You know you don't have to do this," he told her, knowing that this would be completely her decision.

"I know, and this is what I want. We aren't discussing it. I want you to make love to me, and that's what you're going to do."

He raised an eyebrow, a bemused smile transforming his features. "Anything in particular you don't want?" he asked her softly as she came into his arms.

His large hand grasped her around her hip, moving back to palm her ass. Her face went into the crook of his neck, placing light kisses there. She moved so that her mouth was even with his ear. She didn't want to say this too loud, afraid it would ruin the moment.

"Not from behind, that's what he did," she whispered.

"Like always, you tell me if you don't like something that we do. Unless you say something, I'm goin' to assume you're good with it. That's your decision."

She appreciated that. Climbing onto the bed with her knee, she straddled his thigh. To stabilize herself, she brought her hands up to tangle in his hair. He moaned when she pulled slightly on the length there. Keeping his cool here would be the death of him.

"Kiss me," she all but begged him.

His other hand cupped her neck, allowing him to bring her mouth down to his. With small, nipping kisses, he coaxed her mouth open to allow his tongue inside. She tasted of sweetness and something a little spicy, almost like she was just a little bit dangerous tonight.

When he sucked on her tongue, she could feel it straight down to the center of her body. It caused her to flex her fingers against his strong shoulders, allowing her to bring her other leg up so that she straddled him completely.

Afraid she would fall, he brought his hands around to cup her ass, holding her strongly against his body. Pulling his mouth from hers, he ran his lips down her throat, causing her to lean back just slightly. His hands went to her back to brace her, and he buried his face in her chest. Her breasts were full and sat high on her chest, especially at this angle. Her nipple hardened in anticipation as she felt his mouth inching ever closer. She moaned loudly and flexed her fingers as his mouth closed over the hardness there. Her thighs tightened when he applied suction and worried the hard tip between his teeth.

"Don't stop," she breathed heavily.

Without her noticing it, her hips had begun to rock against the hardness at his lap. Shaking, she leveled herself up with the strength of her thighs and pressed his back against the bed, following him down. His lips never left her breast, and without having to hold her, his other hand moved to the other breast, using his long fingers to tease that nipple into hardness.

He made her feel out of control as she rocked her core against him. The feelings he evoked within her made her want to throw every inhibition she ever had out the window.

"Tyler," she breathed loudly as he bit down harder on her nipple.

"I don't know about you," he said as he let go of the hardness with a loud pop. "But I think we just need to get your first one out of the way."

She wasn't exactly sure what he meant until she opened her eyes and saw his index finger go to his mouth. Once there, he licked the tip and then brought that finger to the center of her body.

"Damn baby," he cursed loudly, feeling the wetness there.

With practiced fingers, he ran them between the folds of her body, concentrating on the nub that begged for attention. His other hand continued to toy with her nipple, amazed at how hard it continued to get.

She ran her hands up his chest, frustrated that she couldn't feel his bare skin. That frustration wasn't enough to make him stop what he was doing.

Her hips slammed against his hand as his finger picked up speed on her clit. "What will it take to get you there?" he ground out between his teeth.

"Faster, not harder. Just stay consistent," she panted, canting her hips to go along with his ministrations.

"Do you need my fingers in you?" he asked, obviously not shy when it came to what his lover needed.

"No," she shook her head, it falling back as her mouth opened. "Just whatever you do, don't stop, don't ever stop."

Her hair tickled the small of her back as she threw it back, letting herself go in the throes of the passion he evoked within her.

"Give it to me," he instructed her, feeling her thighs begin to tighten.

Her whole body tensed, and she pitched forward as her release broke through. She landed in his arms, her body still shaking as she came down from her high.

"You are entirely too good at that," she smiled lazily, relaxed now.

He laughed. "I didn't realize there was such a thing as too good."

"You're right," she conceded. "There's not, not at that anyway."

He thought that maybe they were done, but she surprised him when she got up from the bed and walked over to the bag they had bought at the sex store not so long ago. She reached inside and pulled something out.

"What have you got?" he asked, adjusting the hardness that tented his jeans.

"What we need to ease the ache that I still have inside of my body."

He looked as she held up the circle of a condom. Obviously, he was wrong and this wasn't over yet. She stood, her hands on her hips, her breasts jutting out just so.

"I'm gonna need you to take off the rest of your clothes, Mr. Blackfoot. You need to be naked for what I have in mind."

Chapter Twenty-Three

She walked over to where he sat on the bed, his mouth hanging open in awe. Maybe he hadn't expected her to be so forward, but she enjoyed the fact that he seemed to be speechless. Running her hands over his cut, she slipped it off his shoulders and set it with care on the chair that sat near the bed.

As she turned around, she saw his hands go to the hem of the thermal shirt he wore.

"Uh uh," she shook her finger at him. "I get to do this."

"Then by all means, don't let me take anything away from you," he told her, dropping his hands and then using them to lean back with. "Do whatever you want."

Putting her own hands at the hem of his shirt, she ran them up underneath, feeling the warmth and smoothness of the skin there. As she ran them up, she caught the material of the shirt and took it off as she ran her hands up to his shoulders. Appreciation colored her cheeks.

"I never see you work out, but you really do have the body of a God," she complimented.

His laugh was a little shaky. The only thing that told her how close he was to losing his control. "I usually work out at night while you're asleep."

She opened her mouth slightly and then drew her eyebrows together, fixing him with a look that was pure vixen. She gazed at him under her eyelashes. "Invite me sometime."

"Ye...yeah....sure," he stammered.

The fact that he stammered gave her a secret thrill. She had never been one to strike a man speechless, to inspire great amounts of passion, and this turned her on more than anything. Kneeling down in front of him, she went to work on the laces of his motorcycle boots. When he'd helped her get those off, she went to work on the button of his jeans. He lay completely flat on his back because the vision of her kneeling in front of his hard cock caused too many emotions to fly through his mind.

Empowered, she used her finger and thumb to pull the zipper down, making sure to cup her hand around the hardness that she just couldn't ignore. He hissed and ground his head even deeper back into the mattress.

"You are tryin' to fuckin' kill me," he accused her, his accent thicker than normal.

A laugh bubbled deep in her throat. "Only like you try to kill me. Turnabout is fair play," she pointed out.

After what felt like a million years, she had his jeans and underwear off, leaving him exposed. He felt a little shy because of how exposed his emotions were with her, but knew that she felt just as exposed with him. He jackknifed, his abs tightening as she ran her hand down the length of his cock. Her touch was sure and constant, not hesitant at all. That told him more than anything that she really was ready for this. She did know her own mind and didn't need him to make decisions for her.

"You can't play around with me, the way I do with you. Not this first time," he ground out between his teeth. "I can't hold it together," he admitted.

That admission was hot. Knowing just how strong he was and how tight he kept hold of himself told her just how close he was to blowing his top. Opening the condom she'd brought, she pushed it down onto the length of him.

Bringing her knee up on the bed, she straddled his waist. "This is how I want to do this the first time," she told him, her mind completely made up.

"Whatever you need."

She brought her hands up to his and pushed them back against the softness of the bed in order to stabilize herself. He gripped her fingers harder than he would have liked to keep himself under control. As she rose and sank down on his length, they both moaned.

"You okay?" he asked her as she stilled for a moment, closing her eyes.

She nodded. The feelings welling up inside her were numerous. She had known this would bring a lot of them to surface and possibly bring memories that she wasn't ready for. It was a surprise when all she could think about was how good and right she felt with him inside her body.

"I'm good," she told him, a smile on her face.

Tentatively, she began to rock against him, raising and lowering herself in a rhythm that only the two of them knew.

"I'll try not to embarrass myself," he told her, only half joking.

When they got their rhythm down, she let go of his hands, using his chest to brace herself. That allowed his hands freedom to roam, and she shivered as he ran them all over her body. Nothing went untouched by him, her legs, her thighs, her stomach, her back, her face, her breasts. They were all caressed softly as he let her take the lead.

Sweat poured from his brow, and she knew that he was holding back for her. She knew that this pace wasn't enough to get her there, but she just enjoyed it.

"I've never been a more than one time kinda girl," she told him as he closed his eyes.

"With me, one time isn't going to cut it," he promised her.

Just like before, he brought his finger to the core of her body and began rubbing consistently. Not letting up, even when the canting of her hips increased. Her fingers on his pecks flexed and her nails bit into his skin.

"Fuck," he growled, wanting to flip her over and follow the instincts of his body. But with her, this time, he knew he couldn't. "Come for me," he coaxed her.

She really thought that she couldn't. She never had before, especially not with penetration. She just wasn't 'one of those' girls. The orgasm hit her out of left field, and she gasped loudly, digging her fingers into his skin.

"Yeah," he encouraged her. "That's what I want."

When she let out a deep breath, trying to control the beating of her heart, he took it as his cue. Gripping his hands tightly around her hips, he held her in place as he pushed himself deeply into her core at a much faster pace than what she had set.

She wished she could tell him the things that he told her, that she could talk him through it, like he had her. The fact of the matter was though, she had no experience with that.

"Do you want me to come?" he asked her, looking into her eyes.

His were wild, much like she imagined his ancestors were. "Yes," she nodded. "I do."

His body tightened and he pushed his head back, slamming his eyes shut. "Meredith," he breathed, and she felt the surge of his hardness inside of her. She felt the tension leave his body even when he continued to thrust inside her, almost like he couldn't stop.

When he finally did, he gave a soft sigh and opened his arms for her. In a completely comfortable silence, he lay her beside his body and stroked her back until they both fell asleep.

Chapter Twenty-Four

*M*eredith *was running through a dark alley. The ground wet with a recent rain, the smell of garbage pungent in her nose. She didn't know where she was going, she only felt an urgency that she had to get there quickly. Footsteps were coming up behind her, but she didn't know if they were friend or foe. Turning her head to the side, she tried to see behind her, but all she saw was darkness. The feeling of panic began to overtake her. She could feel the person gaining on her, causing her to break into a full-on run. Her arms pumped at her sides, her hamstrings and calves screamed as she pushed herself to go even faster. She looked around everywhere in this never ending alley, trying to find a door to go into. Just as she saw one up ahead, a hand clamped down on her shoulder and she screamed.*

"Mer? It's me, you're okay," Tyler cooed to the woman in his arms.

She had awakened him moments before while thrashing against the sheets, her arms and legs moving like she was running from someone. He saw her eyes widen as she tried to acclimate herself to her surroundings. Breath gushed from her mouth as she tried to slow her breathing to normal.

"It's been awhile since I had one of those," she gasped, hand at her chest over her heart.

"Was it the usual?" he asked, keeping a respectful distance in the bed, just in case this sent her on a downward spiral.

"No,' she shook her head. 'This is nothing at all like any nightmare I've had before. This one almost made me feel like prey to a hunter. Someone was running after me in a dark alley, and I couldn't see them, but I couldn't get away either."

"Do you think it had to do with what we did here tonight?" he asked.

She thought for a moment and then shook her head. "No, I don't. I think it had to do with what I wanted to talk to you about earlier."

"Which was?"

Getting out of the bed, she padded over to where she had put the manila envelopes. It was chilly in the room, so she grabbed the thermal shirt she had taken off of him and put it over her naked body. Walking back over to the bed, she hopped back in and began opening the packages, dumping the pictures all out.

"See, these have pictures in them, and there was one that was sent to my house. It was in storage and I found it when we started going through all that stuff. There are a ton of pictures. Of me, of you, of the club, of Denise, the kids, everyone."

She spread them out between them on the bed and watched as his eyebrows drew together in what looked like anger.

"The fuck? Whoever took the time to do this sure was around a lot. How did we not notice someone following us with a camera?"

This made him uneasy. What else was going on that they didn't know about? Was this someone inside the club? That pissed him off.

"I see you already jumping to conclusions, Tyler. Let's just see if we can find a clue here. Maybe if we can figure out who did this, we can figure out why."

She was right, his anger would get them nowhere. That didn't change the fact that he wanted an explanation and he wanted it yesterday.

For hours they poured over the hundreds of pictures that had been sent to her. There seemed to be no rhyme or reason to them. The only thing that could really be gathered was that someone had unprecedented access to the club and no one had noticed.

"Let's think," Meredith said, putting her reporter cap on. "Who could have done this?"

"I really hate to think that someone I think of as family did this, but it's kind of lookin' that way isn't it?"

She felt horrible for him. He obviously was not taking this well. "If there's one thing I learned in all my years as a reporter and a journalist – it's that not everything is always as it seems. Don't think you've been betrayed by someone you love, let's look at this from all angles. Okay?"

Tyler knew she was right again. Evidence could be made to appear one way when in reality it was a completely different way. It just mattered how one looked at it.

"Do you have a notebook around?" she surprised him by asking.

"A notebook?"

Her smile was saucy. "Yeah, you know one of those old-fashioned things we used to use in school? It's got a wire spiral on the side and these things called lines on the paper."

"When did you become such a smartass?" He didn't skip a beat as he got out of the bed and walked out of the room.

She giggled as she enjoyed the view he presented, both coming and going. Within minutes he walked back into the room, a notebook and a pen in his large hand.

"To answer your question, I think I've always been a bit of a smartass. It's just who I am," she winked.

He leaned over and gave her a lingering kiss on the lips. There was nothing sexual in it, just two people who were comfortable with one another enjoying a private moment.

"We're going to make a list. Ya know, of who could do this. It might be uncomfortable, but we have to know who hangs around this club and had the opportunity to do it."

"As far as hangers-on? All the girls that throw their panties at the guys, especially at Jagger."

She raised an eyebrow in interest. She'd heard Jagger sing here and there every once in a while and he sounded good, but she'd heard that sometimes he went to *Wet Wanda's* and actually put on a show.

"Does he have that many women?"

"Yeah," Tyler nodded his head. "If that boy wanted, he could have a different lady every night."

Curiosity got the better of her. "Does he want one every night?"

Nah, there's this chick at *Wet Wanda's,* but they officially met at the drags in October. She was on the back of a pickup truck where there was a stripper pole. The truck hit a hole, and she bounced out. Apparently Jagger caught her, tits and all. He's been pining after her ever since."

"And you bitched him out, thinking he was after me today? That's just wrong."

"I got my point across though. Didn't I?" he glared at her, not backing down from that argument.

"Anyway," she told him, not wanting to get into it again. "Who else?"

"There's Layne. He started prospecting the same time as Jagger. Jagger's fixing to get a patch, but Layne is further away. There's opportunity there. He's everywhere we are."

With her lip between her teeth, she wrote down the name, along with a couple of the more ardent Jagger Stone fangirls.

"Who else?" she tapped her finger to her chin.

"Everyone else is in these fucking photos."

"Maybe that's it," she stopped shuffling through them. "Maybe they've placed themselves into certain situations so that they'll never be suspected."

"Okay then, who do you think would do something like that?" Tyler asked, almost afraid of what her answer would be. She was way too smart for her own good.

She swallowed hard. This would be suicide if she was wrong. "What about William or Lauren?"

"As in my president?"

"One in the same."

Shock registered on his face. This just couldn't be true.

Chapter Twenty-Five

"How have you been since our last session?" Meredith sat forward in her seat, a huge smile on her face. She had never been this excited to talk to Doc Jones.

"Tyler is no longer sleeping on the floor."

Doc Jones clapped her hands together, excited for her patient. "That's a huge step. How have you been handling it?"

"Not too bad if I do say so myself. I had a nightmare last night, but I don't think it was necessarily because we had sexual intercourse. I think it was something else."

"Define something else."

"I recently decided I want to find out who did this to me."

That was a bomb if Doc Jones had ever heard one. The progress Meredith had made was substantial, but this was more than she'd ever hoped for.

"Are you really sure you're ready for this?"

Meredith nodded, crossing her legs. "I'm as sure as I can be. I'm sick of living with this hanging over my head.

Tyler has promised to help me, and together we're doing this."

Carefully, Doc Jones sat forward. "I caution you again. Do not confuse the feelings you have about your recovery with the feelings you have for Tyler."

She had known this was coming. "I understand where you're coming from, and I can honestly tell you that you're wrong. Even if I never got well, I'd still feel this way about Tyler, and I think he would feel this way about me."

"Is he out there waiting on you?" she asked, pointing outside.

"Yeah."

"Do you mind if we bring him into a session?"

Meredith thought about it for a moment. "No, I don't. Whatever you feel is best. I don't think we have anything to hide from one another. He's already seen me at my worst."

"Tyler, I'd like for you to come in here for a few minutes."

He looked up from where he'd been texting on his phone. It struck him as odd that the doctor would request his presence, but if that's what needed to happen for Meredith, he'd do it. Ambling his way into the office, he had a look at the both of them.

"Please have a seat."

Carefully, he had a seat next to Meredith, afraid that his large frame would break the couch she sat on. "Is this safe," he mumbled to her.

She did her best to withhold a giggle, but it escaped on its own. "Yeah, I think it's okay."

"The reason I invited you into this session, Tyler, is to see where the two of you are with one another. Meredith is very upfront and honest with me, I want to make sure you understand what you're dealing with when it comes to her."

This pissed him off. He saw red and did his best to keep his temper in check. "With all due respect, Doc," he spat the term out like it was a bad piece of food. "I think I'm probably the *only* one who understands how to deal with her. I was the one who found her that night. It was me who took care of her, who held her when she cried, woke her up when she couldn't wake up from her nightmares, and it's me who's promised to avenge her. That's between the two of us, it doesn't have to be approved by you."

Meredith was taken aback by the passion with which he spoke his words. She knew how he felt about her, but to see the way he spoke about it, the way he defended his feelings. It warmed her heart even more.

"I agree with what he said. I don't feel like I have to explain anything. I never set out for any of this to happen. It just did."

Doc Jones smiled. "That's what I wanted to hear. I wanted honest answers, not ones that you had time to cultivate and make sure were just right. I honestly think you're in a good place here and I think he brings out the best in you."

Letting out a breath, Meredith felt like they had passed a test of some sort.

"I do, however, caution you. The closer you get to the answers you seek, the more your memories may flare. You may need to go back to journaling regularly and taking your light sleeping pills. It affects everyone differently. Just be aware of what your body and mind are telling you."

Tyler appreciated the doctor's honesty as much as she'd appreciated his. "Should she come for more sessions? I can make sure she gets here if she needs to."

"That's up to her," Doc Jones smiled. "At this point in time, I think we can move these down to monthly. Unless you have an episode. You seem to be handling yourself rather well."

That meant the world to her. Whether she wanted to admit it or not.

As they approached the clubhouse on the way back, Tyler pulled off to the side of the road and shut the bike down.

"I'm going to take you over to Liam and Denise's. She just got home from the hospital, and I want you to visit with her for a while."

Meredith didn't like what Tyler wasn't saying. "What are you going to do while I'm there?"

He shrugged his shoulder. "Just look around. See what we've got goin' on in the clubhouse. Somebody took those pictures, and I'm going to find out who it was."

She sighed. His mind was made up, and this is what he was going to do. It would do no good to tell him that she didn't think it was a good idea.

"I just want you out of there while I do it."

"Can you at least tell me what you're going to search?" she asked.

He tried his best not to roll his eyes, but sometimes her need to know everything wore on him. "I'm going to try and see if Layne has anything right now. Like I said, I don't suspect Jagger. I'll still take a look at all his stuff, but today I want to rule the two of them out."

"You're scared it's William, aren't you?" she asked, her eyes searching his.

He leaned down, kissing her softly on the lips. "So are you."

She couldn't deny it. He had the power to destroy her, and he'd wanted to before. When she laid out the pros and cons of all the people they suspected, he was at the top of the list. If anyone had a hell of a motive for setting her up and wanting her gone, it was him. He had always thought and assumed she had the power to bring the club down, and maybe she did, but whatever she had – she didn't know it. It was something that he only knew the truth about. Unless he spelled it out for her, she wasn't sure she'd ever know just what she held in her hands.

"You know if it's true, it's going to kill Liam," she fretted.

"Hey," he grasped her around the neck. "If there's one thing I know about Liam, it's that he doesn't stand for lying or women being hurt. If his dad did this, he would want to know."

She did her best to give him a smile, to show him that she believed what he said, but it fell short.

"Let's get you to Denise's. That way if something does go down, you at least have an alibi."

She did not like the sound of that at all.

Chapter Twenty-Six

"**N**ot that I'm not happy to have you here, but what the hell is goin' on with you?"

Meredith looked up from her phone, not sure how long she had been staring at it. Obviously a long time since Denise looked seriously pissed. What Tyler had thought would be an amazing idea had really started to backfire on her.

"What do you mean?"

"You're tense, edgy, distracted. And you keep looking at that damn phone. What the hell is goin' on?" Denise demanded.

Pasting on a happy smile, Meredith shook her head. "I'm not sure what you're talking about."

"Don't use your reporter face on me. Seriously, is something wrong with you?"

It was on the tip of her tongue to tell Denise everything. She wanted to badly. The two of them had confided in one another over so many things since their rough beginnings of friendship. But she just couldn't do it. Not with this. It would put this woman right dead center in the middle of whatever was happening.

"I had a nightmare last night. My first one in a long time." That part was at least true.

Immediately the look on Denise's face softened. "Oh, I'm so sorry. I thought you were moving past that. I really hate to hear it."

"I thought I was to, but maybe some things are just gonna take a little while longer to get over."

Especially the fact that the man who would be your father-in-law may have had me raped. She thought to herself.

"Enough about me, tell me about you. What are your plans now that you're preggers? I know that you had talked about wanting to find a job."

The heat effectively off her, Meredith did her best to concentrate on what her friend said.

"You're right. Now Liam doesn't want me to work. He wants me to stay home in case I have any more complications. He doesn't want me doing anything more strenuous than housework, and that's even debatable."

Meredith cocked a brow. "Lemme guess. You're debating it, and he says it isn't even up for discussion?"

"You know us so well," Denise laughed.

There was a lull in the conversation. It wasn't uncomfortable really, just a lull.

"So does Tyler look as good naked as I imagine he does?"

Meredith spit out the drink of water she had just taken. "What?"

"Oh come on. It's written all your face that you got laid last night. I have pregnancy hormones racing through my body already. Let me live a little."

Touching her chin to mop up the water that had dribbled there, Meredith wondered. Could people really tell she and Tyler had done the dirty? Was it written all over her face? That made her a little uncomfortable and a little proud all at the same time.

"Better," she giggled. "He looks so much better than you think without his clothes on."

Denise joined in the giggling as the two of them settled in for an afternoon full of girl talk.

Tyler almost growled. He was beginning to get very frustrated. He had searched the rooms of Jagger and Layne and come up empty handed. He didn't want to jump to conclusions. In this club, in this life, jumping to conclusions could get a person killed. But he was really beginning to think that his president had something to do with what had happened to his woman.

"Travis," he yelled as he went into the main area where they kept their computers.

"Yeah?" the computer guru asked, coming out from under a group of them, a lollipop hanging from his mouth.

"What were you doing?" Tyler asked as he saw him roll out with the apparatus they normally used to check under cars.

"Really techy shit. Trust me, you don't wanna know. What can I help you with?"

He was so going to hell for this. "William asked me to come get his phone. He's stuck at the shop, and he told me that you were putting a new blocking device on it."

In all actuality, Tyler had heard this news in passing a few days ago when he'd been at the shop. It was William's personal cell phone, and as such he didn't want anyone to be able to track him unless he wanted them to.

"Yeah, here ya go," Travis reached over to a box that held a ton of cell phones and pulled one in particular out. "Tell him that he'll need to reset his passcode. I had to change it in order to make the necessary changes to the phone."

Tyler grinned. "Will do."

He walked out of the clubhouse normal as could be, hopped on his bike, and drove it a few miles down the road before pulling over to the side. A stand of trees provided him a little bit of privacy as he began scrolling through calls made and texts. There were a few numbers that he called more often than others. He quickly transferred those numbers to his phone, along with a few names and a few email addresses. He realized very quickly that everything older than a few days was gone from the phone. It was obvious William kept his phone clean.

Changing the passcode to something he could remember, he started up his bike and drove towards the shop. The ride to get there seemed to take forever. He hated suspecting someone that he respected so much of something so heinous as rape. Even if he had ordered it, that wasn't how Heaven Hill worked. As he pulled into the parking lot, he saw William's bike there. Parking his and shutting it off, he made his way into one of the bays that housed the cars they worked on.

"Hey, pres, got somethin' for ya."

William looked up from where he was changing spark plugs on a late model car. "What's that?"

Tyler held up the cell phone and flashed him a smile. "I saw Travis at the clubhouse. He asked me to bring your finished phone to you. He had to put a new passcode on it to download the information. I wrote it down for you and stuck it in your case," he explained.

Grabbing it, William nodded a thank you and went back to his work, never questioning why Tyler had it.

Walking back over to his bike, Tyler had a seat on it and stared straight ahead. His mind worked a million miles an hour. Since he had the passcode, he could look in that phone at any time. In days, the answer to what had happened to Meredith could be theirs. Now, however, he wasn't sure he wanted to know the truth anymore.

Chapter Twenty-Seven

"That must be either Liam or Tyler," Meredith commented.

She and Denise had taken up their favorite spots in the house. Out back on the screened in porch. Being November it was a little cool, but Liam had outfitted a space heater for the area and blankets kept them plenty warm. It was beautiful, especially with night falling.

"Could be both," Denise yawned, covering her mouth with her hand.

When the front door opened, they heard a virtual stampede of feet on the hardwood,

"We're back here," Denise yelled.

In an instant two teenagers and two bikers were also in the back room.

"Hey, baby," Liam greeted. He leaned down to give Denise a kiss. With a soft touch, he caressed her abdomen before straightening to his full height. "So I was tellin' Tyler that it would be a good night to cook out with everybody here."

"Oh that would be fun," Meredith smiled.

The kids seemed to be in agreement as well.

"Why don't you two do your homework real quick and take your showers. I can smell you from over here Andrew," Denise laughed. The young man had football practice every day, and it was obvious in the way he'd bulked up how hard he worked.

"I know mama, I can smell myself."

"Tyler and I will go fire up the grill."

Meredith got up from where she sat. "I'll go make the sides. You just stay right there little mama."

Denise pouted. "Can I at least come sit and talk to you?"

"Sure, but you aren't lifting a finger."

"I gotta talk to you about something," Tyler said, his voice low as the two of them started grilling hamburgers and hot dogs.

"Sure, what is it?"

Tyler had grappled with whether he should tell his friend what was going on or not. It could put them all in a bad situation, but Liam was his oldest friend. He and his father had never seen eye to eye and Tyler knew that the two of them were more like family to each other than any blood relations they ever had.

"I hate to tell you this," Tyler sighed, running a hand through his hair.

It was obvious his friend was struggling. "Whatever it is, man, just spit it out. The two of us have been through some shit. There ain't nothing we can't tell each other."

"But I don't want to tell you this."

"Ty, when have we ever lied to each other?"

He knew the answer to that. Never. That's why they were such great friends. That was why they trusted each other so explicitly. In this life, you had to have that one person who would look out for you no matter what the cost. They were that person to each other.

"I think William ordered the rape on Meredith."

Liam's head visibly kicked back as if he'd been smacked in the face. "Wow. You sure?" His mind went back to the events weeks ago, when William had made Meredith public enemy number one as far as the club was concerned. It wouldn't be that far of a stretch if he had ordered it, but it still didn't feel good to think it was the truth.

"All signs are pointing to yes. Do I want it to be true? Fuck no."

Liam knew that Tyler would never make an accusation like that without at least having some information as to why it would be true. Tyler had always been honest and fair, almost to a fault.

"You know whatever it is, true or not, I'll stand behind you."

That meant the world to Tyler. "I'd understand if you didn't. That's your dad."

"But you're the one who's always been there for me. No matter what. Family is family, and blood don't make you family."

Tyler pulled the other man into a hug. "That means a lot to hear you say that. You know I don't have loyalty to many and I don't trust many. I value you and your opinion on anything and everything. Later on tonight, I'd like to talk to you about what I'm thinking. I just don't want the ladies to be involved. This can't come back on them."

"Agreed, brother, agreed."

"How was football practice?" Tyler asked Andrew as they all sat around eating dinner.

"Hard," he admitted as he swallowed a bite of hamburger.

"You're on the JV team right? That's pretty good for an eighth grader."

Andrew couldn't keep the happiness off his face at the praise of the other man. "Yeah, they say I'm big enough."

"I did the same thing in middle school. I had to drop out of high school in tenth grade, but I was a beast on the football field. You need to start bulking up a little bit. You don't wanna be a lanky guy like him over here," Tyler grinned over at Liam.

"Fuck you, man. Not everybody can look like they came out of *Muscle Magazine.*"

Denise whistled. "Hey, language. We're gonna have to watch that with the new baby."

Tyler cleared his throat, a grin on his face. "Anyway, Drew if you feel like it, you can come work out with me sometime. I work out at night, but I can do it in the morning if that would be better for you. You've got the height, you need the muscle mass."

"That's what coach said, and I asked Liam if he'd come work out with me, but he said he really doesn't," Andrew rolled his eyes.

"Hey, at least I'm not lyin' to you. About the only working out I do is workin' on the cars and riding my bike."

"Yet you somehow seem to be blessed with a bangin' body," Denise stage whispered.

"Mooommm," Mandy groaned.

"If you don't mind, I'd love to come work out with you," Drew effectively ignored everything else at the table.

"Alright, you wanna go in the morning or at night?"

"Morning. I have practice every afternoon, and I don't think I can give it 100% after practice."

Tyler smiled at the boy. "That's a damn good attitude to have. I'll meet you tomorrow morning at 5 am. If we run late, I'll take you to school."

Meredith watched the exchange, something soft and sweet in her eyes. This man was so much more than she had ever imagined. He had so many facets to his personality. Many that she was sure she hadn't even witnessed yet. It made her want to witness them. It also caused her mind to wonder. Would this be what he was like when they had a teenage boy to raise?

Later on, after the kids had gone to bed, they all sat in the living room talking like couples do. When there was a lull in the conversation, Tyler made eye contact with Liam and motioned towards outside.

"You wanna go take a smoke?" Tyler asked.

"Yeah, let's go. Ladies, it's a bit chilly out there. We'll be back in a few minutes."

Once outside, they had a seat on the front porch, each lighting up their respective vice.

"So tell me what you know so far."

"Fuck man, I'm not even sure where to start. There's so much shit going around in my brain right now."

Liam blew out a steady stream of smoke from his mouth. "Just start at the beginning."

So he did, explaining to Liam about the envelopes with the pictures and the fact that the person would have to have unprecedented access to the club. "That's when I automatically thought Layne or Jagger. They are new and we don't know a whole lot about them, I figured it would be easiest to suspect them. I searched their rooms, but couldn't find shit. That's when I thought about William."

"Let's think about this. What would he have to gain by getting back at Meredith?"

"Motive. She was getting awfully damn close to breaking open all our secrets before she was attacked. I mean we all said that she was like a dog with a bone. All of us avoided her, and let's be truthful, even we don't know about the skeletons in this club's closet from way back when. Your dad is the last remaining of the first five. He can manipulate anything that he wants."

"You do have a point there. A damn good one. So what have you done?"

"I got his phone's passcode. I took down a few numbers, and I'm going to see if Meredith recognizes them. I have a feeling one of them might be one of her informants for the other clubs from her reporter days. I'm going to try to get into his network and download his old messages too. He may have a sim card somewhere. You never know."

"You know this could mean death, right brother?"

Tyler swallowed hard. "I've never feared it before. Why start now?"

"You've got someone who depends on you now."

"If I don't get to the bottom of this, I will never forgive myself. If I do and it kills me, then I will gladly go as a martyr. I just hope that you'll take care of her if something does happen to me."

That thought caused Liam's stomach to churn. There was no way he wanted to think of that, but he of all people knew the life they led. "You don't even have to ask. She's in good hands if this all goes south. I'll give my own life for that."

That was all Tyler needed to hear. Now he wouldn't rest until he found out the truth and God help the person that stood in his way.

Chapter Twenty-Eight

"**D**o you recognize any of these numbers?"

Meredith looked at the numbers that Tyler had written down on a piece of paper the next day, trying to remember the numbers she had used in her investigations. She pointed at one. "This one looks vaguely familiar. They were all disposable prepaids, I'm sure. I had them written down in one of my notebooks. It would be in my desk if I remember correctly."

They went to the room that housed her stuff. She made a beeline for the desk and reached into the bottom drawer, pulling it out of the wood structure. Reaching inside, she engaged a lever and a false bottom opened, revealing some paper work.

"That's pretty hot that your desk drawer has a false bottom," Tyler grinned. "Means you're mysterious and dangerous."

"If only," she giggled.

Going through all the information she had, she pulled out a small black book. "This has all the phone numbers I used. Let's see."

She went through them as he looked over her shoulder. "There," he pointed. "That one is the same. Who was that to?"

He watched as she swallowed loudly. "That was my contact for the Vojnik. The one who didn't show up that night." Her face became deathly pale, and she ran for the bathroom, throwing up everything she had in her stomach.

Tyler was torn between following her and trying to decide if he should leave her alone. Wanting to be near her won out, and he ambled into the bathroom, wetting a washcloth for her. He sat next to her on the floor, pressing the coolness to her forehead.

"You okay?"

"No," she whispered, her voice shaky. "I've lived here in this clubhouse with that man for months. He's smiled at me and told me he thought I was better." Tears came to her eyes, and she angrily pushed them away with violent strokes of her fingertips. "This whole time…he knew."

An anger that Tyler had never felt before washed over him in waves. He wasn't sure how to control this anger. Earlier in life, he would have gone out and found a fight, beating another man until he almost died. At this point, he was ready to admit, he was too old for that.

"I don't want to stay in this clubhouse with him anymore," she declared, holding her arms across her stomach.

"I don't either," he admitted.

That was the bitch of the whole thing. If he wanted to prove that William was behind this, he would have to stay. He would have to collect evidence and keep his head down. Maybe they would have luck for once and the man who raped her would appear. Now that they knew who ordered it, Tyler knew the guy had to still be around. William demanded loyalty and ease of access. If this man had done this once, William would require him to do something equally heinous again.

"What do you want to do?" Tyler asked, his voice hoarse. It felt like she was leaving him, and his breath came in great gasps. His hands shook and he felt sick to his stomach.

"I don't want to leave you," she cried.

"But you feel safer doing that." He finished for her.

"Could I go to your house?" she asked, tears streaming down her face.

Her world was crumbling again. She had thought that she had found a home here, a place to belong. And now it was being taken away from her. Everything that she thought was the truth was just an illusion.

"No," Tyler cupped her face in his hands. "None of what you and I have shared has ever been an illusion."

She must have said that out loud, but she didn't remember it. That was the scariest thing of all. This had thrown her completely off.

"I care about you, Mer, I'm never gonna let anything happen to you again."

She closed her eyes, reveling in his hands on her face. She wanted to believe him. With everything she had, she wanted to believe that he *could* keep her safe. Never before this had she ever thought he *couldn't*. But now she had doubts. Now, she wasn't so sure.

"Don't do this," he begged her. "I can see you shutting down on me right now. This isn't changing anything between the two of us. This is just a temporary roadblock. This is nowhere near the end of us."

Tears spilled over her eyes again, and her face screwed up in a look of utter despair. "Then why does it feel like it is?"

"Because you've had a shock, baby. I'm not letting you go," he promised, putting his arms around her. He held her so tightly against him that his muscles shook.

"Neither one of us knows the future," she argued.

"I do, and mine is with you. I understand that you need some time. I get that. I'll put you up at my house. Give me a few hours to get Travis over there to wire some security for you. William doesn't know about that house, so you *will* be safe there. I'm warning you, I'm not giving up on us. Don't you give up on us."

It felt like such a hopeless situation to her. Things had changed on her in the blink of an eye, much like it had the night she'd been raped. It felt like the biggest setback of her life.

"I think I need to call Doc Jones," she whispered.

"If that's what you need to do, then by all means do it! Do you need me to take you there?"

She hated this. She hated pulling away from him and seeing the hurt in his eyes, but he was too close. He was too close to the hurt, too close to the danger.

"No, I can take myself," she whispered, trying to ignore the pain in his eyes.

He knew her well enough to know that she'd stubbornly dug her heels in and she wasn't budging. "Let me at least give you my truck. It's got a tracking device on it, that way I know where you are if I need to. You haven't driven your own car in months, who knows if it's ready to be driven. It's winter and it could snow. Let me put you in something that I know you're safe in. At least give me that much."

"Okay," she agreed.

He reached into his pocket and pulled a key ring out. Handing it to her, he smiled sadly. "I was gonna give this to you tonight anyway. It's keys to my house and truck. Anything that's mine is yours, and I wanted you to know that. Go get your stuff together, and then I'll show you which truck is mine."

Grateful for the exit strategy, she ran from the room before she could sob. Life wasn't fair, and it had never been more unfair than at this exact moment. Haphazardly, she threw articles of clothing into her bag. It didn't matter if they matched or not, she just wanted out of this clubhouse. On her way back out of the room, she noticed one of Tyler's hooded sweatshirts sitting on the dresser. Pulling it up to her nose, she realized he must have worn it recently because it smelled like him. Without another thought, she put it into the bag along with everything else.

"You ready?" he asked as she walked out of his room.

"As I'll ever be."

He grabbed her hand as they walked out of the clubhouse. They made their way to the garages that housed club members' cars, and he opened the one that had been deemed his. A very manly black Chevy stood in front of her. Dark window tinting and chromed out, it fit him like a glove.

He opened the door for her and helped her in before throwing her bag into the passenger seat. Using his large hands, he turned her to face him and stood between her parted thighs.

"I'm not letting you go, I hope you know that. I understand why you have to go for now, and it's breaking my heart, but I do understand."

She took a shuddering breath. "You're way more than I deserve, Tyler Blackfoot."

"That's where you're wrong. I'm exactly what you deserve, and I'm not letting you forget it. I'll give you a little bit of time, but be prepared. I'm not leaving you alone. I understand that you need to come to grips with this, but expect me in a few days." He leaned in, giving her a soft kiss.

He shut the door before she could say anything else and tapped the window to let her know it was okay to leave.

Putting the key in the ignition and driving away from the clubhouse was the hardest thing she'd ever done in her life.

Chapter Twenty-Nine

"**M**eredith, I'm surprised you called me so soon."

The next day she was in Doc Jones' office, breathing deeply and trying to control the emotions that had plagued her all night. "I was too, to be honest with you."

"What happened?"

"You cautioned me about trying to find who did this. You told me that I may not like the answer and that it may bring up other things. I foolishly thought you were just being overly cautious," Meredith explained, tears already coming to her eyes.

In the past eighteen hours, she'd tried to stop the emotions. She had tried to stop the crying, but she just couldn't. She couldn't deny the depths of the feelings she had for Tyler and how it had broken her heart that she'd left him.

"I take it you found out something that has been difficult for you to comprehend?"

"What we talk about here is privileged, right? You don't discuss this with other people?"

Doc Jones took her glasses off and sat forward in her seat. "I'm bound by federal patient confidentiality laws Meredith. What we say here will not go beyond these walls. That is one thing I can promise you."

She took a deep breath and forged on with the story of what had happened. "We found out that William Walker, the President of Heaven Hill, might have ordered the rape on me."

Sitting back and breathing heavily, she reacted. "That's a hell of a shock."

"You're not kiddin'. I've lived with that man since it happened. I've been alone with him on numerous occasions. I'm best friends with his would be daughter-in-law. I feel so stupid and betrayed."

"Those are not uncommon feelings, Meredith. You're justified in what you feel."

It helped to have someone vindicate what she felt, but it didn't shake the loneliness or the sadness that had plagued her since she'd left Tyler in her taillights.

"So because that is William's clubhouse – I left it. I left Tyler there and told him I couldn't stay anymore."

The sympathy was immediate in Doc Jones' eyes. "That had to hurt both you and Tyler deeply."

"It did – it has," she cried. "But I just don't know how we get past it. William is always going to be there unless we can find a way to bring him down. I have this feeling of utter despair right now, and I saw the anger in Tyler's eyes. It was murderous. I don't want to be the reason he's angry."

Her mouth set in a thin line, Doc Jones took a deep breath. "Do you really think you're the *reason* he's angry, Meredith? Do you really think he's angry *at you*?"

"I know he's not angry *at* me, but I don't want to cause him to have feelings that might get him in trouble."

"That's what you do when you care for someone. You stand up for them, and you tell the world that they are yours. That's what he's doing. Don't punish him because he cares for you. You would do the same for him if the roles were reversed."

Meredith knew that Doc Jones was right. If someone had hurt Tyler, she would be the first person in line cussing and throwing punches at them. It was just hard to deal with, the fact that she'd lived with such rose-colored glasses on.

"I guess I'm angry with myself," she whispered.

"Okay, now we're getting somewhere. Why are you angry?"

"What kind of a person lets themselves be used like this? I made myself a pawn in a game that I knew would have no winners."

"But you never asked to get raped, you never asked to be beaten. You cannot take the blame for what others did to you, Meredith. That's not the way to handle this. Do not let these people off the hook. They did something wrong and they must pay for it. Remember that *you* are the victim here."

Meredith heard everything that the doctor said, but it was hard to let go. She still felt responsible.

"I can see it in your eyes. If you feel the need to be responsible for something, take responsibility for the fact that you started the game. That *is* something you can take responsibility for. Know that you've learned a life lesson that many others have to learn over their lifetimes. But

99% of the people who learn this lesson are not raped. Let yourself off the hook for that."

Breathing came a little easier as Meredith thought about what the doctor said. Letting herself take responsibility for some portion of this made her feel better. It didn't completely absolve her, but it did give her purpose. It did give her a feeling of contentment.

"You're right. I'm glad I called you, I do feel better taking responsibility for my role. I'm gonna have to do some groveling with Tyler. I completely pushed him away."

"You were trying to protect yourself, and Tyler probably understands that," Doc Jones patted the other woman's knee. "He has great insights on the human psyche."

"That he does, especially mine. I'm sure he'll forgive me, but I'm a little embarrassed to face him again."

Doc Jones waved a hand in her direction. "Things can't be perfect all the time, and it's good for your relationship if you have a few disagreements here and there. You know what they say about making up."

A blush rose to Meredith's face. "I don't know really, I've never made up with anyone before. I'm really out of my element in all of this."

"Then let me tell you, woman to woman. You enjoy the making up. That's usually why couples fight."

Meredith left her session with the doctor feeling like a completely different person. Instead of the flight feeling that had overwhelmed her the night before, she was back in the fight mode. She wanted to fight for her relationship, fight for justice, and fight for truth. She wondered if she should go to the clubhouse and see Tyler, but realized that he might need some more time to himself. The look in his eyes the night before had told her just how much she'd hurt his feelings.

Pulling into the driveway of the home she'd stayed in, she sighed. What she wouldn't give to be coming home with Tyler there every day, every night. He had so quickly become a fixture in her life that it was scary, but she knew after her night without him, she needed him. She needed the stabilizing force he brought to her. It had quickly become something that she couldn't live without.

Walking up the front porch steps, she put the key into the lock and turned it, opening the door and walking in. She gasped as she glimpsed Tyler sitting on the couch, looking like he had not a care in the world.

"You scared the ever-loving shit out of me," she gasped, putting her hand to her wildly beating heart.

He got up from the couch and silently walked over to her. When he got so close her back pressed against the door, he put his hands up beside her head and shoulder, effectively boxing her in. A devilish glint in his eye, he leaned so that his mouth was even with her ear and whispered.

"I told you that I wouldn't let you get away. I've given you a night, and now I'm here to tell you one thing. Don't ever run away from me again."

She moaned and closed her eyes. Without a doubt, she was in so much trouble.

Chapter Thirty

Tyler took his hands from the door and ran them down her body.

"I told you I wouldn't let you run away from me," he told her again.

"I know, and I'm sorry I ran," she whispered.

Her eyes were still closed and that bothered him. "Open your eyes and look at me."

She followed his order, and the look there stole her breath. It was so intense that she wanted to close her eyes again.

"Keep them open," he instructed her. "Look at me, see what I'm telling you."

The only thing she could do was nod.

"No matter what happens or what we find out, it's not going to change how we feel about each other. We have to promise this to each other. I know that it's not going to change how I feel about you, and I think you feel the same. We can't let outside forces change the way we live our lives. There will always be outside forces if we let there be."

She knew that he was right, everything about what he said was the truth. Couples faced challenges every day and they didn't run from them. The ones that lasted stayed and fought.

"You're right. I want this to last, I don't wanna give you up."

He put his hands at her waist and squeezed roughly. "Then fight for me."

She put her hands on his shoulders and hopped up, crossing her ankles at his back. "I *am* fighting for you. I'm doing the best I can, but I've never had anyone to fight for before."

"You have me now."

She grinned saucily at him before tangling her hands in his hair. "I do, don't I?"

"Don't forget it again."

Leaning forward, she took his lips with hers. His lips were always so soft, no matter when she kissed him, they were always full and kissable. Tilting her head so that they could remain connected, she coaxed his tongue out of his mouth. He relaxed against her, allowing their tongues to stroke against each other.

His hands trailed down her back and stopped when he got to her thighs. Gripping them with strong fingers, he hiked her up higher, making her bend her head to continue kissing him. It gave him an advantage when he widened his stance and pressed her harder against the door. Letting go with one hand, he brought that hand up to the middle of her chest. He broke the kiss as he hooked his index finger in the gap of the button down shirt she wore.

"Do you like this shirt?" he whispered.

"It's not a favorite. Why?" she was confused. Why were they talking about this now and not continuing with the slow screwing against the wall he was obviously teasing her with.

"Just makin' sure."

With that, he gave a tug and the buttons gave way as the shirt hung limply from her body. It was on the tip of his tongue to ask if she had been okay with him doing that. If it caused any bad feelings because her breathing had picked up speed, but he was silenced when she attacked his neck. He moaned, feeling the little nips of her teeth and then the soothing coolness of her tongue against his flesh.

The same finger he'd used to rip the shirt from her body made its way to where her bra encased her breasts. Softly, he pulled the cups down under her breasts, effectively trapping them together. As she continued to work on his neck, he swirled his tongue around the hard peak of her nipple.

Her fingers gripped his shoulders as her core started a slow rock against his. This was different compared to how they always were. Everything in their lives always needed to be done right this instant, and in this they could take their time. His strong arms bulged as he took her weight off the wall and walked them over to the couch. She loved to watch the strength there, the corded muscles and the thick forearms as he performed any kind of task.

Tapping her thigh twice, he motioned for her to unwrap her legs and then helped her down. Not saying anything, she closed the distance between them and made short work of his cut as well as the shirt he wore underneath it. He stood in just a pair of jeans and his motorcycle boots. Without a shirt on, she could see all of his tattoos and for the first time, she took the opportunity to look at them. Some were MC related, others were obviously related to his culture. As she ran her lips around the circumference of his frame, she noticed one that gave her pause. On his left shoulder a dream catcher, inked in grays and blacks, had the date of her attack in its netting.

"What's this?" she asked, running her fingers over it.

He turned so that they could see in each other's eyes. Sometimes things like this made her feel like they were an old married couple. Other times, he continued to amaze her.

"It's there to remind me of the night my life changed forever. And I'm not sure if you're familiar with dream catchers, but they are supposed to keep the bad dreams at bay if you put them over your bed. I figure if I have you in my arms, those dreams get to me before they get to you. I want to stop them before they start."

From any other man that would have been ridiculously clichéd and just a line to get in her panties. But not with this man. Anything he said, whether good or bad, he truly meant. Coming back around to the front of his body, she stopped and took a deep breath.

"I really don't deserve you," she whispered, burying her head in the curve of his neck and nuzzling there.

"You do deserve me. We deserve each other. There's a reason I found you that night," he told her.

His deep voice told her not to question his words, so she didn't.

With more grace than she felt, she ran her hands along the waistband of his jeans. Once her fingers got to the metal button, she lowered her eyes and ran her tongue along her lips as she unfastened it. The tines of his zipper were loud in the quiet room as she fought to bare him to her eyes. After she pulled his underwear and jeans down, he sat on the couch to rid himself of the boots. While he did that, she worked on ridding herself of her remaining clothes.

When he was done with his boots, he hooked her around the waist and pulled her to straddle his lap. He could feel the trail of moisture she left on his thighs as she situated herself over his girth.

Fumbling with the jeans he'd put beside him, he pulled out a foil packet and suited up. Once the barrier that protected both of them was in place, he used the head of his cock to tease her with just a few quick strokes against her clit.

She ground her body into his, sighing as he seated himself completely inside her. This was getting easier, she realized. Being with him like this. She was starting to crave it, the intimacy and the closeness. Grabbing his hands, she used them for leverage as she gained speed to her rhythm.

Growling at her abandon, he buried his face in her neck. He wanted to mark her, show the world that she was his. Nipping at the sensitive skin just below her ear, he sucked strongly, hoping to leave his mark there.

"Ty," she gasped as he soothed the sting with a stroke of his tongue.

"I want everybody to know you're mine," he told her, untangling their hands and then burying his in her hair. He pulled her close to him so that every inch of their bodies touched.

"I am yours."

And with that promise, he pushed them both over the edge.

Chapter Thirty-One

Hours later, the two of them lay tangled up in the sheets of his big bed. A cold front had moved through, bringing with it a steady rain that pelted the tin roof of the farm house. Because it was older, it was also drafty. Laying together, sharing body heat under the covers seemed to be the best way to spend the rest of their day.

Meredith sighed as she entangled her leg with his and scooted closer to the warmth of his body. She lifted her head as she raked her nails across his stomach. "What are we going to do about William?"

That question had been on the tip of her tongue the entire time they had been here together, but she hadn't yet wanted to break the spell they seemed to be under.

His large hand grabbed hers at his stomach, stilling the motions she made there. Turning it over, he brought the palm up to his mouth and brushed a kiss there on the delicate skin. "I put a passcode on his phone that I can get into. Right now, the only thing we *can* do is wait and see if he continues to contact that number. It's the only proof we have he's involved."

She hated that answer because that meant she would more than likely have to go back to the clubhouse. "I figured you would say that."

"I'm not askin' you to do something you don't wanna do, baby. If you don't wanna stay in the clubhouse anymore, then we won't. We'll stay here if you want."

"How does that work, Tyler? You're an officer. This is too far out for you to be riding back and forth all the time."

He knew that she spoke the truth, but he would still do whatever would be easiest for her. "Relationships are about compromise," he shrugged.

"Compromise, yes. Giving me my way, no," she argued.

"I don't see it as you getting 'your way'. You don't feel safe there. Who am I to tell you that you have to stay?"

The words that were coming out of his mouth gave her the warm fuzzies, but she knew they were not realistic. It was time for her to put on her big girl panties and deal.

"You're right, I don't feel safe with him there. But with you by my side, I know that no one will hurt me. I can't run from this my whole life. I either take a stand now, or I let it rule me. That is a choice I have to make."

His hand tangled in her hair as he pressed slightly against her neck, meeting her halfway for a kiss. "You truly are one of the bravest people I've ever known," he whispered.

"I don't feel brave. I feel scared shitless."

His deep laugh warmed every part of her that was chilled by the thought of going back to the clubhouse.

"That's understandable. You never know. Maybe it will put pressure on him, seeing you every day."

"He's seen me every day since the attack that I've been there. I don't think William Walker gives a shit."

A slow grin spread over Tyler's face. "He's seen you and we've seen him, but we haven't really expressed to him how we feel about you being raped. Now have we?"

"I don't think I'm following."

"By the time I'm done with him, he's going to regret the day he went after you. If you think the 'curse of the skull cup' was bad, you ain't seen nothin' yet, baby."

That thought scared her and thrilled her at the same time. "Can you please just leave Jagger out of this one? He really was just doing me a favor."

"Yeah, I'll leave him alone. Even though it's obvious you have a soft spot for the boy," he growled.

She giggled, running her hand up his stomach to his throat. There she caressed his Adam's apple and ran the tip of her nail to his chin. "Don't be jealous, Tyler. It doesn't become you."

His eyes took on a predatory gleam. "Oh, I'm not jealous. Any man who sees you in the next couple of weeks will know you're spoken for."

"What do you mean?"

"You have a hickey the size of a half dollar on your neck. It's a beauty if I do say so myself," he grinned in a way that told her just how happy with himself he was.

She groaned. "Oh Tyler, now I'm gonna look like a waitress from *Wet Wanda's*."

"It's hot and I think it makes you hot, whether you wanna be straight with me or not."

He was so full of himself, lying next to her with a huge grin on his face.

"I'll wear a turtleneck," she threatened.

"The hell you will," he fired back, leaning over her body to admire his handiwork.

"I might as well have a tattoo on my forehead that says 'Tyler's woman'."

His grin was dead sexy. "We can arrange that. It would be considered a true honor by my people."

"Now you're just being sarcastic," she poked him in the stomach.

"That hurts," he complained when she poked a little too hard at his ribs.

"Poor baby," she cooed. "Maybe I should kiss it and make it better."

"Maybe you should."

The smile she flashed him was pure feminine affection and appreciation all rolled into one. Pressing him flat on his back, she leaned over and placed soft, soothing kisses where she had poked her finger. He lay back, enjoying the attention she gave him. All of a sudden, she sucked on the smooth skin there, leaving a bruise almost immediately.

"There," she smiled when she came up for air. "I marked you too."

"I'll wear mine like a badge of honor. Not like a two bit hooker at a titty bar," he quipped causing her to yelp and reach out to pinch to the spot that she had just marked.

Holding her wrists back, he laughed at her attempts to overpower him. "Watch your knee," he laughed, when she continued to struggle against him.

It was futile. He was almost a foot taller than her and outweighed her by over a hundred pounds. Breathing heavily, she gave up the fight. "One day, Tyler Blackfoot, you are going to regret that remark," her voice held great promise.

"I'm shakin', baby. Can't wait to see what you do."

Liam sat on the back porch of his home also enjoying the rain, along with a cup of coffee. He did some of his best thinking on this porch – in that, he and Denise were very similar. He had woken early this morning and taken the kids to school, not wanting them to stand out in the rain waiting on the bus. When he had gotten back to the house, Denise was still asleep. Since he hadn't been put on the schedule for Walker's Wheels, he had this whole day to himself.

He was moody today, still pissed over the information that Tyler had given him about his father. It was no secret that the father/son relationship between the two of them was tenuous at best. The person who had really been mother and father to him had been his sister, Roni. He had never really cared what the biological parents ever thought, only what Roni thought. He couldn't deny that this hurt though. It was like William was two different people. A Dr. Jekyll and Mr. Hyde. He preached loyalty to the club, but he violated it when he went after a woman that would be an old lady someday. It made him wonder what he really would have done to Denise if he hadn't stepped in when he did where she was concerned.

"Goddamn it," he swore, running his hands over his head and letting it hang.

"What's the matter?"

That soft voice got him every time. In a world that bordered on insane, she grounded him like no other person could. Without saying anything, he reached out for her and sat her on his lap. More than anyone besides Tyler, he trusted her.

"Tyler told me that he thinks Dad ordered the rape on Meredith."

Tears sprang to Denise's eyes, and he cursed again.

"I didn't tell you this to upset you, honey."

"I'm pregnant," she sniffed. "I'm emotional."

"I'm sorry that I don't know how to deal with these hormones," he apologized.

"It's okay, tell me everything."

He related the story to her and watched as her face went from one of complete devastation to one of complete anger.

"How could he do that and look at her every day?" she whispered, running her hand along his shoulders.

"I don't know. He's a different kind of man than I thought he was. That's for sure. It makes me sick that I'm his family. It makes me sick to think of what he could have easily done to you."

"Don't drive yourself crazy. We can't worry about the past and we can't change it, but we've got to make the future better. We're about to have three kids in this family and the members are starting to settle down. If this club is going to be successful, we need to make changes."

He knew that she was being honest, but he wasn't exactly sure what to do about it. "I know, we need to make some plans."

Maybe it was time for him to plan his ascension to the top.

Chapter Thirty-Two

"You think Rooster will help us?" Tyler asked as he and Liam sat outside the Sheriff's office downtown.

"I think it's worth a shot," Liam answered.

They were taking a huge chance, sitting just off of the historical downtown area of the square, their bikes parked at an angle on the street. Every officer that came out wearing the brown of the Sheriff's department gave their bikes and their cuts a once over. Liam was pretty sure that everyone knew who they were. The two of them sat in silence, watching each officer that came out of the building. When they noticed the red head of the man they wanted to see, Liam whistled and motioned for him to come on over.

"To what do I owe this pleasure?" he asked as he walked over. The loose-hipped way he walked belied the turmoil he felt inside.

Liam took off his sunglasses and leveled his old friend with a stare. "We need some assistance for old times' sake."

Rooster didn't like the sound of that, in fact it caused sweat to break out on his brow. "Is this gonna be illegal?"

"Not all of it, and I think you might remember how much you owe me."

This intrigued Tyler, he had never heard much of the story involving the old friends. He filed that away to ask about later.

Rooster's face got red enough to match his hair. "What do you need?"

This is where Tyler took over. "I need a dump on William's phone. I set up a passcode on it, but it's not working the way I want it to. I want numbers, texts, GPS locations. It's an iPhone, I know it can be done, but you need a subpoena for what I need."

Rooster widened his stance and crossed his arms over his chest. "You mean to tell me your hacker can't get you what you need?"

"Not all of it. There's some kind of security glitch on it, and honestly, I'm trying to keep this quiet."

"What exactly are you lookin' for here?"

It was on the tip of Tyler's tongue to lie, but he felt that maybe in this moment with this person who looked to be willing to help them – the truth would set him free. "I'm positive he ordered a rape on someone I care deeply about. I want his balls in a noose for it, but I can't make a play without the correct information."

"Now I can't condone you killing somebody."

"Never said I'd kill him. I will tell you this though, whatever you wanna do to him is fine with me when I get done with him. I have a feeling William Walker has many more secrets that none of us know about."

Liam picked up the conversation. "I'm givin' you a little professional courtesy here. When his ass gets taken down, I'm takin' over Heaven Hill."

Rooster did his best to digest all the information that had been given to him. When push came to shove, he really did owe Liam. "Y'all are gonna have to give me a little bit of time. I think I can work it, but I'll *have* to get a judge to sign off on it. I have to have some sort of investigation going on."

"Don't insult my intelligence," Tyler laughed. "There's *always* an investigation going on with us."

Rooster noticed his supervisor coming out of the building and put on his sunglasses. "That's my boss. I gotta go, but I'll be in touch. I'll do what I can," he said before walking off and getting into his cruiser.

"We just need to keep going, business as usual," Liam advised Tyler who nodded before they started their bikes and rode off.

The next morning, Tyler woke up at 4:30, groaning at the alarm. Meredith groaned as well.

"Why the hell is that thing going off so early?" she grumbled, putting her pillow over her head.

"I promised Drew we'd start working out together the other day and then flaked on him. We're starting this morning. You want to come?" he asked as he left the warmth of bed and stepped into a pair of sweatpants and a hoodie.

She thought about it for a few moments.

"Last chance, I'm outta here, we're meeting outside to do a warm-up run."

Running was something she hadn't been doing nearly as much of and she missed it. "Oh alright, let me grab my stuff."

Ten minutes later the three of them stood outside in the darkness of the morning. She shivered and stomped her feet, trying to stay warm. Their breath could be seen coming out in big white puffs.

"Let's go," Tyler said, bringing his hood up over his head, instructing them to do the same. "Retain what body heat you can, you want to sweat to warm those muscles up. If I go too fast for either of you, let me know. I got long legs, and I'm aware that makes it a bit easier for me to run."

"If you guys take off without me, it's fine," Meredith said. "If you get out of my line of vision, I'll yell."

They nodded and took off, following Tyler along the property. Thirty minutes later, she and Drew were both huffing, having fallen a bit behind. Up ahead, they saw they were almost back to their starting point and Tyler was waiting on them.

"Keep it up," he clapped, encouraging them to finish strong.

"C'mon, Mer," Drew said, kicking it up a notch.

She couldn't let these two men outdo her. From somewhere deep inside, she pulled on a reserve that she didn't know she still had, and the two of them finished neck and neck. They both bent over at the waist, sucking in gasps of air.

"Walk around with your hands on your head," Tyler instructed. "It's cold, that may help you get some more oxygen in."

The two of them did, laughing at each other. The looks on their faces were identical.

"You," she panted, looking in Tyler's direction, "are in much better shape than I thought."

He grinned as he leaned down to brush a kiss along her wet forehead. "Gotta be to keep up with you, woman." Glancing over at Drew, he winked. "See, get in as good of shape as me and you can get a woman as hot as that."

Embarrassment covered Drew's cheeks in bright splotches. "I'll keep that in mind," he stuttered.

"Let's move inside to your garage. Liam moved all my weights up there."

Drew took off ahead of them, and Meredith leaned over to pinch Tyler's arm. "Don't embarrass him like that."

"Baby, he was checking you out! You are hot, and I'm sure you're going to fuel all his teenage masturbatory fantasies. He's a boy."

She laughed, rolling her eyes. "Oh my God, I'll never be able to look at him again."

"It's natural. I promise. Razzing him will make him work harder because now he'll want to impress you. He's gotta get some weight on him or he's gonna get hurt out on that football field."

She sniffed at his know-it-all tone. "I guess if you say so then it must be true."

"Now you're learnin'," he put his arm around her as they made their way into the garage and began the second part of the workout.

Later on that afternoon Meredith made her way stiffly back to the Walker household. Denise had invited her to lunch, and she had jumped on the offer. Especially since Liam and Tyler had been called out for a protection run.

"Hey," Denise greeted as she made her way into the house.

"Hey," she winced, walking through the living room and into the kitchen.

"What's wrong?" Denise laughed as she stiffly sat down at the kitchen table.

"Tyler is a slave driver. If your son is walking around like he's not sore this afternoon, I might kill him," she grinned.

Denise whistled. "Tyler didn't get that to-die-for body by just being blessed like Liam was."

"Oh. My. God. Are you checking out my boyfriend?" she accused, pointing a finger at her friend.

"Did you finally put a label on it?"

Meredith stopped and thought about it for a moment. "I guess I did. We've never called each other boyfriend or girlfriend, but I know I feel more for him than friends with benefits. I know we're both committed. That's what that means right?"

"That is what that means. I'm glad you're comfortable enough to *put* a label on it. You've really come a long way, Meredith. I'm proud of you."

Uncharacteristic emotion clogged up Meredith's throat. "Thanks, I think I'm proud of me too. Now I'm hungry. What are you feeding me?"

Effectively moving the conversation in a different direction, the two of them spent the afternoon just enjoying each other's company. If nothing else came of this horrible time in her life, Meredith knew that she appreciated the friendships she'd gained and the relationships she'd cultivated.

Chapter Thirty-Three

"I've got the information you need."

Liam had suspected it would take a lot longer than a few days for Rooster to obtain what they wanted, but he had really come through. "Where do you want to do the drop?" he asked through the cell.

"Our old hang out." With that, he ended the call.

Liam hung up and motioned for Tyler. The two of them were on repo duty with the wrecker, and it would be the perfect excuse for them to leave. "Rooster just called. He's got our information. In a few minutes, act like you got a text with a tip on a car. We need to head out towards Richardsville."

Tyler nodded and a few minutes later did exactly what Liam had asked of him.

"We're headin' out," Tyler called out to William, who waved before they left with the wrecker.

As they rode out to the old Garvin bridge, Tyler pulled his bottom lip in between his teeth.

"You nervous?" Liam asked.

"It sounds weird, but yeah, I am. I'm nervous that I'm right, and I'm nervous that I'm wrong. How crazy is that?"

"Not crazy at all, I feel the same way," Liam admitted. "We're not gonna know until we get the information and really look at it."

"I need you to make a promise to me," Tyler said as they turned onto Garvin Lane and headed for the bridge.

"What's that?"

"If we find out that he really did do this, don't let me kill him. I can with my bare hands, I know this about myself. Just make sure you save me from me."

"I promise, but I can't promise I won't kill him."

The two of them pulled up near the bridge and came to a stop when they saw the Sheriff's car and Rooster leaning against the hood. He waved at them as they parked on the seldom traveled road.

"Thanks for this," Tyler told him as they walked to meet him.

"There's useful information in there for me too, don't make me better than what I really am. I do hope this helps you get some closure to it," he said handing them a large manila envelope. "I was even able to get pictures, and I don't think you're gonna like what you see, but you asked for it."

Tyler's gut churned. He wasn't sure which one of them Rooster was really talking to, but either way, he had a feeling this wasn't good. In minutes, the transaction was complete, and the two men sat in the wrecker with the information that could either clear or convict their President.

"What do you want to do with this?" Tyler asked, the manila envelope feeling very heavy in his hands.

"We keep it between us, and tonight Denise and I will go over to your house for dinner. I know that's not your normal MO and you want to keep that place private, but we need to do this somewhere that's out of the way."

Tyler nodded. "You're right. I'll call Meredith, and I'll have her make a big deal out of it. Have her take my truck and act like it's a huge deal. Actually, I won't tell her what we have until after we eat. You do the same with Denise. I'll have Meredith take her over there."

The two of them agreed and set their plan into motion. Liam called Roni and asked her to get the kids for the night. He had a feeling this was going to be long and more emotional than any of them had counted on. He needed to keep them safe and out of the way.

Meredith had a feeling that something was up. Without a doubt she had been completely surprised when Tyler called her and told her to go all out for dinner. In his truck he instructed her to open his glove box, and in it had been a debit card with her name on it. He had told her to buy a dinner and anything she needed to cook it with. And also whatever she needed to make the kitchen feel homey.

She had never had a home before, always lived in an apartment, so this was exciting. She and Denise had gone all over town. The mall, the little shops downtown looking for fresh flowers and silverware along with dishes and table cloths. She had picked out new curtains and a few knick knacks that made a house a home. After going to the grocery, the two of them drug everything inside, and Denise went to work setting up the stuff they bought while Meredith went to work on the food.

"This house is super cute," Denise beamed. "I never would have thought of this for Tyler, at all. He really is surprising. I'm beginning to wonder what else I don't know about him."

"He does have a lot of facets to his personality," Meredith agreed. "It scares me sometimes, but I know with him usually what you see is what you get. I do wonder what the hell is going on tonight. He was so adamant about this being for him. Liam's apparently only been here once or twice, and now he's asking me to host both of y'all for dinner."

"That is a bit odd," Denise nodded, putting the fresh flowers in a vase they had purchased.

Hours later, the food was finishing up as Tyler and Liam pulled into the driveway. They walked in together, both sniffing the air at the same time.

"Something smells fucking fantastic in here," Liam praised as they took off their shoes and jackets.

"Hopefully you'll like it," Meredith grinned, walking over to give Tyler a hug.

His stomach growled loudly. "I'm pretty sure I'll eat it and love it if my stomach is any indication."

"You're cold," she accused, as he wrapped her in his arms.

"It's a little over a week to Thanksgiving. I *should* be cold," he laughed, walking into the kitchen to wash his hands.

Liam followed suit before grasping Denise up in a hug. "This place looks great, really, you've done a lot of work in here Tyler."

"Thanks, it's been a slow go, but it looks really nice tonight. The two of y'all did an amazing job with the stuff you bought."

Meredith felt a rush of pride and was happy to know that he liked what she had picked out. "I'm glad you like it. We've been smelling this food all afternoon, let's eat."

As she said that the timer went off, and she moved over to the oven and pulled out a cast iron skillet. "Is that homemade cornbread?" Liam asked, his eyes wide.

"Sure is."

"I love you in a purely platonic way, but just know that I love you," he grinned, already walking towards where she had sat it on the stove.

A Dutch oven sat on one of the burners. "What else do we have?" he peered inside, groaning. "Seriously? Homemade pot roast and cornbread? I'm in heaven."

Tyler shot him a glare. "Quit flapping your damn gums and get the food so the rest of us can eat too. I'm just as hungry as you are, damn."

The ladies laughed as they went back and forth with each other before they all sat down together at the table. Dinner was comfortable with the four of them, like it always was. Numerous times throughout the meal, Tyler and Liam had exchanged glances, almost like they didn't want to look at the information that had been given to them. They seemed to be having too good of a time.

Tyler and Liam cleared the table and put away the leftovers while the girls washed the dishes they had dirtied up. Afterwards, they all had a seat at the kitchen table again, drinking coffee and just talking.

"Why did you really invite us here?" Denise asked out of the blue. "I'm a mother, and I've noticed the looks that the two of you have been shooting at one another all night. I've seen those looks before between the twins. Why don't you just be honest with us?"

Tyler swallowed hard. He didn't want to ruin the easy camaraderie that had developed over the night, but he didn't want to lie to them either.

"We talked to Rooster the other day. We asked him if he could get us a complete dump on William's phone. That meant text, pictures, calls, emails, GPS locations. He was able to get us what we wanted, and he gave it to us today. Liam and I want to be straight with the two of you, and we thought we should go through it together. We had to get somewhere that William couldn't just walk in. So we chose here."

Meredith felt a lot of the warmth that had seeped into her bones leave, but she understood this and the reason for it.

"Well what are we waiting for?" she asked. "Let's do this."

Chapter Thirty-Four

Meredith sat in shock as she watched a video of the night of her attack. In the envelope there had also been a USB Drive. She hadn't been sure she had wanted to see what it held, but knew that after all the other incriminating evidence they had viewed, it had to be something big. Someone had been in the bushes that night filming, they had heard her scream for help and hadn't come to her rescue.

Denise choked back sobs as she held onto Meredith's hand beside her. "Let's turn this off," she pleaded.

"No," Meredith stopped her. "I have to see this. I have to see what he saw while he heard me screaming for help and didn't come to my rescue. I need to know what kind of a bastard he really is."

"I've seen enough," Tyler whispered, getting up from the table and making his way to the other room.

He had a seat on the couch, putting his head in his hands. Most of the information they had received had been text messages and voice mails that detailed the planning of her attack and set up that would bring the club down on her. What William hadn't counted on was the depth of

Tyler's feelings for her, that was apparent. He had a need to kill William. To feel his bones break and to see the blood pour from his body.

"You okay?" Liam asked as he walked over to carefully sit next to his friend.

Tyler's temper could sometimes get the better of him. The beast could sometimes come out, and Liam knew it was close.

"Not at all. I want to murder your father, my President, with my own two hands. I want to slowly put knife marks in his body and let him bleed out a painful death. I want to take the guy that did this and cut his cock off so I can shove it down his throat."

"We *have* to sit on this. We still don't know who the guy is that actually raped her. We get both of them at the same time. Otherwise, William will tell him and let him run."

Tyler knew the words Liam spoke were truth, but it didn't make anything easier.

"That was the most disgusting thing I have ever seen in my life. The fact that a man can sit by and watch as a woman screams for help while her body is violated…" he stopped and took a deep breath. "I just can't fathom it."

"That's because we are way better men than my father will ever be."

Liam sensed he needed to turn this conversation onto another direction or things would get very dark in his friend's head. "We need to figure out what to do about the other information we found. He's been playing both sides of this goddamn protection business. Getting paid by us and then getting paid by the Vojnik on the runs he leaks the information to. No wonder these trucks need protection.

The Vojnik know exactly what's on them and where they're going."

Tyler leaned his head against the couch. "There's not a damn thing we can do tonight. We need to think about this carefully, and we need to figure out *who* actually raped her before we go pointing fingers."

"Agreed, we go on with life as normal as possible. You keep that savage temper of yours under control."

"I will," Tyler promised. "I'll do it because I want justice for her. I want her to be able to feel comfortable again, and that won't fully happen until we find this fucker."

"I'm trusting you, Ty. You keep your shit locked down."

"I know."

Liam got up and went back to the kitchen, collecting Denise.

After they left the house filled with a thundering silence. It was so loud it roared in his ears. He didn't know what to do, what to say to Meredith. Before, when he hadn't *really* known what had happened, it had been easier. Now, he just wasn't sure how to approach her.

An hour later, she walked slowly in the living room. Her face was pale, her eyes red. He opened his arms to her, and she collapsed next to his body.

"Are you okay?" she asked him.

His laugh was hollow. "I should be asking you that."

"I lived through it once. You, on the other hand, had never seen it. I'm sure it was a shock."

He cleared his throat. "It was a lot more savage than I thought. A lot more violent. You're so well-adjusted now, I just thought it was different. If that makes sense."

It didn't really to her, but she decided to just overlook that. It was obvious he was still trying to come to grips with what he had seen on the video. "I'm that well-adjusted because of you. You've made me who I am today. I can never repay you for that."

"Yes you can," he told her, tightening his arms around her. "Don't ever leave me."

She smiled up into his face. "I hadn't planned on it."

The two of them sat in silence, enjoying each other's company. After a while, she turned to face him. "How do we play this? Now that we know he ordered this. What do we do?"

"I know you're gonna hate hearing this, but we're going to act like nothing has changed. We can't let him suspect we have this information. If we let on that we do, he could tell your rapist and then he could run. I don't want that. I want the pleasure of the kill."

She nodded, understanding why they wanted to play it like this and even looking forward to it. Over the past few weeks, she had decided that enough was enough. "I want that too."

Acting like nothing has happened is driving me nuts. I even started packing the gun that Tyler taught me how to use. I carry it with me at all times. It's small and couldn't kill anyone, but it gives me peace of mind. I know that both Tyler and Liam believe that it's what's best for now, but I would give anything to let William know just how precious his time left here is. I want to see Tyler beat the shit out of him. Maybe I'm beginning to become a little savage myself.

"You're coming to my show right?"

Meredith glanced up from her journal into the mischievous eyes of Jagger. "What show?"

"I'm playing *Wet Wanda's* the day after Thanksgiving, it's gonna be bigger than normal. I'm officially inviting everybody."

"Like with a band and everything?" she asked, excited for the young man she had come to know so well.

"Just me and my guitar. I'm a little nervous. I'd like for you to be there."

She had heard him humming around the clubhouse, singing softly to the radio every once in a while. He did have a good voice. She was excited for him. "I will *totally* be there. I'll get Tyler to come too, and he can muscle my way to the front row."

Satisfied with her answer, he grinned, already looking for something else to do.

"What was that about?" Tyler asked as he had a seat next to her, putting his big arm around her shoulders.

She sank into the weight, welcoming it. "Jagger is apparently playing a show at *Wet Wanda's* the day after Thanksgiving. He wants me to come, and I want you to use those big, powerful muscles to get me up front." She emphasized the words big and powerful with a breathless voice.

"Oh, you're good," he grinned. "You know I'll do anything you want me to do."

"Great. Then it's a date."

He liked the sound of that. "Sounds like a good time."

"Anytime I get to spend with you is a good time. Speaking of time spent together, can we go to the dorm room for a minute?"

He lifted his eyebrows up seductively. "Yeah? It's the middle of the day."

She hit him in the stomach. "Not for that. I want to talk to you about something."

Without a word, he grabbed her hand and led her to the room that he called his. Shutting the door, he put a finger to his lips and then pulled out a device she had seen him use a couple of times. In minutes he'd swept the room for bugs.

"We're clear, what's up?"

"I had an appointment with my therapist this morning about the video. She wanted me to ask you something."

"What's that?" he asked, having a seat. The mention of the video still made his gut churn and still made him want to kill someone.

"Do you need to go talk to her? Alone? You know, about what you saw?"

That question floored him. He was actually speechless. He struggled to answer it.

"I mean, I don't wanna put you on the spot. But I know it was a shock to you, and I know you weren't expecting it. I wouldn't think less of you if you wanted to talk to her. She just wanted me to throw that out there to you. It doesn't matter to me what you decide."

He realized that she was doing this for him, and that made his heart swell. "After this is over, I think I will. I think we both should together. But I wanna keep this anger for now."

She could appreciate and live with that.

Chapter Thirty-Five

Thanksgiving

"Are you going to be okay doing this?" Tyler asked as he and Meredith got ready for the big Thanksgiving dinner with the club.

"I could ask you the same thing, as well as Liam and Denise. Things are going to be fine," she assured him.

Thanksgiving dinner was a huge tradition with the club. Given that so many of them came from broken homes, a lot of members wouldn't have a place to go for the holidays. So the club provided the traditional meal.

"Are you sure you don't want to go visit *your* family today?"

Meredith shook her head. The love she saw amongst this group of outlaws was more than she had seen in her family in a long time. "No, the only thing my dad's going to ask me is if I've decided to put the college education he paid for to use again. My mom will just sit there and nod. I'd much rather stay here."

Tyler didn't have family, so he didn't really understand the dynamic. "If you say so."

"I do."

They made their way into the dining area of the clubhouse. The large table that could hold everyone sat decorated, and Meredith had to hold the intake of breath. They really did go all out for this. They had good plates as well as tablecloths on the table. Each chair had a place setting, and it looked like there were even linen napkins as well. She noticed that every place setting had a cup except for Tyler's. Jagger caught her eye and winked.

"If you want your mug, you're gonna have to get it yourself."

The group laughed, remembering the 'curse of the skull mug'. Tyler's laugh was full bodied, and she thought she saw tears at the corners of his eyes. They all had a seat and started passing around the food. Once everyone had their plate full, William stood at the head of the table.

"It's a tradition here at Club Heaven Hill every Thanksgiving, we go around the table and tell what we're thankful for. I'll go ahead and start. I'm thankful for the prosperity of the club, and the fact that we've continued to stay relevant in a changing political and economic climate."

Up next was Liam, who cleared his throat and put his arm around Denise's shoulders. "I'm thankful for my new family and the friendships I've been able to maintain. Without that, my life wouldn't be anything, and this year I figured that out."

It went down the line to a few more people when it came to Drew. He fidgeted in his seat, playing with this glass. "What are *you* thankful for?" Denise asked, looking at her son.

"I'm thankful for Tyler agreeing to work out with me. I'm thankful for the new brother or sister I'm going to have. I'm thankful for us coming to this place. We've never really had a family before, and I've never had a dad before. I'm glad I have one now."

That took the breath out of everyone. He had never called Liam Dad before, never even mentioned it.

"You sure?" Liam asked, shock and pride apparent on his face.

"I am, we both talked about it. You are our dad no matter what," Drew motioned to Mandy who nodded.

She was the quieter of the two and almost always deferred to Drew when things like this came up. It was so good to see her agree.

"I've been calling you my kids to everyone but the two of you, so I'm glad you think of me the same," Liam choked out.

He stood up and went around the table to hug both of them. Everyone watched the group, happy that so many had found happiness in their situations this year. The table came around to Meredith and Tyler.

Meredith cleared her throat. "I'm thankful this year for the trials and tribulations I've had. They've made me appreciate the good times, and they've brought me to this place and to this man who I care about more than I can say."

Tyler wanted to tell William exactly what they knew and that he should enjoy his last holiday here with the club he supposedly loved so much. But he couldn't bring himself to do it. Not with the kids around and not before he had a chance to exact his revenge. "I'm thankful also for the universe bringing me this beautiful woman."

Everyone raised their glasses in salute. When he saluted his, he looked straight at William, a smile on his face.

The group at the table sat around eating dessert and drinking coffee a few hours later. William had made an abrupt exit, and Liam got up on the pretense of having a cigarette. Minutes later, he texted Tyler to let him know that an unknown car had come to pick William up and had driven off down the road. Liam texted the license plate information to Rooster, hoping he could run a search on it. Everyone else went on with business as usual.

Beside him, Meredith crossed and uncrossed her legs, turning to face Jagger. "Did you invite everyone tomorrow night?"

"What's she talking about?" Steele asked.

Jagger's face turned red. "I hadn't, but I guess I will now. I'm playing a show at *Wet Wanda's,* and you're all welcome to come if you want." Even though he had played shows there before, he'd never actually invited everyone. This would be big if they all came.

"I've heard you sing when you think no one is around. You're not half bad. I'll be there," Travis told him, nodding in his direction.

A couple of the other guys agreed, promising him they would fill the place up.

"No pressure or anything," Tyler grinned, looking over at the younger man. "My lady has informed me that you're good, and I'm muscling us up to the stage, so you better not disappoint."

"Motherfucker, that's a lot of pressure," Jagger ran a hand through his hair.

Meredith smiled prettily at him and waved. "Aren't you thankful I came into your life?"

The guys laughed as he shifted, uncomfortable. "You are going to get me killed by your boyfriend over there. That is, if I don't die of nervousness first. Damn, I need a cigarette." With that, he got up, almost running for the door.

"You've got him all tore up," Tyler laughed, taking a drink from his infamous mug.

"I like to keep him on his toes. He's fun to pick on," Meredith shrugged. "That being said, I expect to see everybody at his performance tomorrow. It means a lot to him, whether he admits it or not."

"Yes ma'am," Liam saluted as he made his way back to the table.

He motioned to Tyler to check his phone. The name had come back from Rooster as well as a photo of the license of the person the car was registered to. When he opened the cell, he knew without a doubt something was wrong. The picture was of an African American man. They knew that the man who had raped Meredith was Caucasian. They had to do something and fast. They both knew that William could be on to them, and that would be a very dangerous situation.

Chapter Thirty-Six

Meredith screamed along with the other women who surrounded her. She wasn't exactly sure what it was about a man playing guitar that women loved, but it was downright sexy. Never had Jagger looked more at home than he did up on stage. She really couldn't believe this was the same man who was scared to death of the curse of the skull cup. She'd heard him humming and singing to himself a few times, but she'd never known his voice was so rich. As the crowd began to surge closer towards the stage, Tyler wrapped his arms tighter around her body. No one was getting in between the two of them, no one would separate them. She put her hands over his and squeezed, showing her appreciation of the fact that he wouldn't let anyone encroach on their space.

The fact that she was even in this crowd, not freaking out, was amazing. After Jagger's set, she turned around and motioned for him to bend down so that she could talk into his ear.

"I'm thirsty," she shouted.

Her voice was hoarse, and he had to concentrate to hear her.

"You want me to go get you somethin' or do you wanna come with me?"

She loved the spot they'd claimed at the side of the stage, they could see everything. However, her calves were starting to hurt, and she needed a break from the crush of the crowd. She knew another band would be playing after Jagger, but really he was all that she had wanted to see.

"I'll go with you."

He turned around, grabbing her hand with his large one. She grabbed onto his cut as well, knowing that no one would touch it and they wouldn't get separated in the crowd. Following him as he bullied his way through the crowd, it wasn't long until they broke the edge and she could finally breathe again. Even though it was winter, the crush of bodies had made it extremely hot and humid.

"You alright?" he asked as they emerged from the crowd.

"Yeah, this was great," the smile on her face warmed his heart. She'd been around all these people and not had a panic attack or been uncomfortable once. He was prouder of her than he'd ever been of anyone else in his life.

Directing her towards the hallway where they were selling concessions, he saw Liam who'd also headed out of the crowd.

"Had to get out of there. Was starting to get nervous with all those people at my back," he said as he walked with them towards the concessions.

"Me and you both," Tyler agreed.

They stood in line waiting for it to be their turn to be waited on. "What do you want?" he asked as they realized they were next.

"Bottle of water is fine with me," Meredith said.

He directed her over to his other side so that he could grab his wallet out of his pocket. She watched as Liam told Tyler what he wanted as well and then came to stand next to her. It was on the tip of her tongue to ask how Denise was doing since they'd all left her alone for the night. When she went to turn, she bumped into another hard body and turned to apologize.

"Sorry," she smiled at a tall man who milled around her.

With this many people, she knew that it wouldn't be out of the realm of possibility to run into others. He smiled back at her, but the look on his face gave her the chills. His eyes were familiar, but she couldn't place it. She grabbed Liam's arm and stood closer to him.

"You okay?" he asked quietly.

"That guy just gives me the creeps," she whispered back to him.

While he waited for Tyler to pay for the drinks, he put his arm around her protectively. If she felt uncomfortable after everything she'd been through, there was a reason for it. Tyler turned to them, and she could see confusion on his face as he saw Liam's arm around her.

"Sorry, she was feeling uncomfortable."

"It's okay," Tyler said, grabbing her chin in his hand. "You alright?" he asked her, a softness in his eyes.

"Yeah, I just got a little creeped out when a guy bumped into me."

Immediately, he was on the offensive. He realized that she had felt fine in the audience full of people, but one man made her feel on edge. He strongly believed in feelings, and obviously she was having them. So was he. It centered in his gut, and he couldn't shake it. This meant something. "Point him out to me," he directed.

She turned around in circles, looking for the man who'd given her that feeling. He wasn't going back to the concert, so she turned towards the exit. "There he is," she pointed him out as he walked towards the exit.

"Let's go," he instructed. He had a feeling about this one. "Liam, don't leave us."

His tone said not to question him, even though Liam ranked higher in the club. Liam didn't hesitate to follow.

"Be quiet and don't ask questions," he instructed her as they followed at a distance and watched the man walk around the building.

Tyler increased his speed as they continued to follow. Just then the man's cell phone rang, and Meredith stopped in her tracks. The sound of the little girl on the ringtone singing Happy Birthday to her daddy made her blood run cold.

When he realized she wasn't walking with them anymore, Tyler looked back at her. The look on her face said it all.

"That's him," she whispered, her body shaking. Her teeth chattered as the shakes went through her.

"Wait here."

She wanted to tell him not to do this, not to hurt this man, not to get himself in trouble. But she knew that he had to avenge her. Another side of her wanted him to do that.

"Go after him," she yelled at Liam. "Don't let him kill that guy."

A part of her didn't want to watch this, the other part of her couldn't do anything *but* watch.

"Hey motherfucker," Tyler yelled as he ran to catch up with the guy.

Spinning around, the guy questioned him. "Who you callin' motherfucker?"

Without answering, Tyler grabbed him up by the neck and slammed his body against the hard brick of the building. "You don't know me, but I know you. I will kill you," he seethed quietly. "A few months ago, you raped a woman. That was my woman, and you will fucking pay for it."

Tyler had to give the guy credit, he didn't get scared. He actually smiled. "And it was so good too. I wish I would have had more time. She was a hot piece of ass."

Rage tore through Tyler's body so strongly that he knew he could snap this guy's neck in half with no effort. Instead, he began pounding on him. The tear of his knuckles felt good as he hit him repeatedly in the face. When he'd beaten him enough so that the other man slumped to the ground, he started in with his feet, kicking his ribs repeatedly. Breathing heavily, Tyler knew he should stop, he was taking this too far. His hands ached, his back ached, his legs ached, but he couldn't stop. He kept seeing Meredith that night in his mind. How she'd looked when he'd found her in the parking lot. The way she'd looked when she'd woken up from all the nightmares.

"Get the fuck up!" he yelled. "I'm not done with you."

Out of nowhere, Liam came up behind him and grabbed his arms. "I think both of you have had enough," he said quietly.

Unbeknownst to him, tears had run down his face, and he wore the other man's blood on him. Lifting his hands up to his eyes, he wiped at the tears quickly, hoping that no one had seen his show of emotion.

"I'll have Jagger take care of him. We'll take him to the garage and get him to talk. You go take care of Meredith."

Shit. She'd seen that. She'd seen him lose complete control over his temper. He hadn't done that in years. He needed a minute to gather himself. Leaning against the wall, he rested his head against it and fought to regulate his breathing. He fought to shut the door on the beast inside him. He hated to let it loose, and he didn't know how Meredith would react to him now. He'd been so intent on his goal that the other man hadn't even gotten a shot in. Closing his eyes so he could breathe, he inhaled deeply. Out of nowhere, arms went around his waist.

"You okay?" Meredith asked, her voice quiet. He hated that.

"I'm fine," he strangled out around the lump in his throat. "Sorry you had to see that."

"Are you kidding? Nobody's ever stood up for me before like that. I love you for that."

That hit him in the chest like a brick. They'd never shared those words with one another, and the fact she did it after witnessing that meant so much more. The tears that he'd shed before came back with a vengeance.

"Turn around and look at me," she told him, trying to turn him with her own strength.

"Let me get a hold of myself."

Out of Darkness

"No, I want to see you. It's alright if you're showing emotion, Tyler."

He turned around to face her, tears still streaming down his face. When she saw him, the tears that she'd been holding back came unchecked. Wrapping her arms around him, she buried her head in his chest, holding on for dear life. He held her just as tightly as she held him. When he finally felt like he was over the flood of emotion, he pulled away from her and framed her face with his hands.

"I love you too. There's absolutely nothing in this world I won't do for you. You don't have to worry any-more because when we're done questioning him I'm gonna beat his ass to death."

Liam and Jagger ran up to them, grabbing the man up by his shirt. Tyler could have been breathing fire with the look on his face, and he turned to Liam, knowing this was it.

"Call your dad and get his ass in on this too. Tonight we finish this."

Meredith had never been so scared of what was going to happen in her life.

Chapter Thirty-Seven

The entire club had gathered at a warehouse that they owned next to the Barren River. The man that Tyler had beaten sat in a chair, arms tied behind his back, feet tied to the legs.

"What did you call everyone here for?" William asked, as they all assembled.

Liam walked towards the group milling around the doorway. "Please, allow me to explain. This man is the man that raped Meredith. It was a horrible crime, one that affected everyone in the club and our significant others. We've all talked over the past few months of what we would do when we found that man."

"Yeah, we'd kill him," Steele agreed.

Jagger stood on the same side as Liam and Tyler, flanking the man in the chair.

"Well, we found him," Tyler pointed at the man sitting in the chair. "The bitch of it is that one man in this room paid this piece of shit to rape the woman that I love. He set up the whole thing."

Shouts erupted as each of them began pointing fingers at the other.

Tyler whistled loudly, getting everyone's attention. He went over to where the man sat in the chair and pulled his head back by the hair on his head. Blood poured from his nose and mouth. "Would you like to tell everyone who hired you?"

The man tilted his chin towards their president, blowing the cover on the whole thing.

"Seriously?" Steele asked, backing up from where he stood next to William.

"There were choices that had to be made. I made them," William defended himself.

Tyler took off and grabbed William by the throat, shoving him up against a wall of the warehouse. "I thought of you like my father for the longest time, and then I find out that you've done this. I want to kill you, but I don't know if I can." The inner turmoil was apparent on Tyler's face and his blood thundered in his ears.

"I did what I had to do for the club."

"The fuck you did. She didn't know anything really, you could have scared her. You didn't have to have her raped and beaten."

"She was a threat," William argued.

"She wasn't a threat after old Dickie boy was dead. Yet, you still kept going."

"You and I both know she never would have stopped. She wanted to break this wide open. She had my secrets at her fingertips whether she knew it or not. Meredith would have known if she looked hard enough."

"Known what?" Liam screamed. "What was so fucking important that she couldn't find out?"

"That you're not my son," he whispered. "Your mom is a whore and cheated on me. You are not mine, but I paid her back didn't I? You've been my bitch most of your life. You even carry my name." His grin was triumphant. "I knew that if these men knew you had no loyalty to me they'd leave me and go with you. This club is all I have, and she threatened that. My livelihood was going to be gone if she told you. I know you. You would have taken your mother's side because she fed you all that bullshit about how she really wanted you when you were a child. You've always done what I wanted you to – even when *you* didn't want to. If you follow me, then they do. If you don't, then they push back. I'm not an idiot, you're my golden ticket with these men."

That revelation didn't shock Liam as much as it should have. Rage and hurt did make an appearance, but he put it tightly under lock and key. This wasn't about him. This was about Tyler and the woman who'd had her innocence shattered by a bastard with a vendetta.

"She would have backed off if you would have just scared her. You didn't have to ruin her life to do that," Tyler's grip tightened on the older man's neck.

"C'mon Tyler, show me some of that savage mentality that we all appreciate so much." He reached into his wallet and pulled out a dollar bill, flinging it in Tyler's direction. "You wanna hurt me son? Hurt me. I'm not one bit sorry for what I did."

Bringing his forehead close, he banged it heavily on William's nose, feeling the bone break and blood spurt onto his face.

"Motherfucker," William groaned.

Tyler leaned in close. "I want to mop the floor with your brains, but I don't want that on my hands tonight." Leaning back, he spoke louder. "You're no longer my president, and you're no longer fit to run this club. I say we take a vote right this fucking minute. Who's with me?"

The group was loyal, but William knew they were no longer loyal to him. Somehow in all of the time he had used plotting, these men had become loyal to someone else. It was apparent they were now loyal to Tyler and Liam. He looked around as all of them raised their hands in a show of support.

Looking over at Liam, Tyler motioned for the knife he carried in his pocket. Liam threw it and watched as Tyler cut the President patch off the older man. "You aren't fit to wear this anymore." He tossed the patch to Liam and nodded his head. "Looks like your *boy* is about to take his rightful place at the head of this table. Any objections?"

Not one person raised their hands. Tyler walked over to his best friend. "It's up to you what we do with him, but that piece of shit sittin' in that chair is mine."

Liam nodded as Tyler stalked over to the man in the chair. He pulled his head up so that they looked at one another. "Make sure you get a real good look at my face."

"Why?" the man asked, his words sounding muffled because of the swelling of his lips.

"It's the last thing you're gonna see." Tyler's ravaged hands pulled out the gun he carried on him and put the barrel to the side of his head. Without a thought, he pulled the trigger, exhaling as the feeling of revenge went through his body. That feeling settled deep in his stomach. It felt like he could breathe again. The first real breath he had taken since Meredith had been attacked.

"Get on outta here. We'll take care of everything else," Liam told him.

Without a look back, he exited the warehouse, got on his bike, and headed for home.

Meredith sat in Tyler's dorm wringing her fingers together. Denise had offered to let her stay at her house, but Meredith had wanted to know as soon as Tyler came through the doors that he was safe. This is the part she hated about this life – waiting on him to come home, wondering if he was dead or alive.

She knew that if she would have been asked months ago if she would be one of those women who would sit around waiting on this, her answer would have been a resounding 'no'. Things had changed in her life in so many ways that she hadn't been prepared for. Some for the worse and some for the better. She knew without a doubt the feelings she had for Tyler were the best.

The door to the room opened, and she saw the man who had made everything right come through it. He was walking stiffly, and she knew the punishment he had put his body through this night had been completely for her.

"You okay?" she asked him.

"I'm hurtin' pretty good, but it's over. You don't have to worry about that piece of shit anymore. I'm not sure what Liam is doing to William, I left that up to him, but your rapist is gone."

A sense of peace settled over her, one she hadn't felt in months. "I know I shouldn't be glad that another human being is dead, but I am," she whispered.

"I am too," he admitted.

She watched as he went around the room, taking off the clothes he wore and then immediately went to the shower. He was quiet, too quiet, and she was worried. Taking off her own clothes, she followed him, getting into the small space behind him.

"I can understand if you look at me differently," he told her, not turning around to face her.

"What nonsense are you talking about?" she asked as she put her arms around his waist and hugged him to her.

"You saw me beat a man almost to death tonight. I'm not going to lie to you, I shot him in the head, in cold blood. This is the man you've been taking to your bed. How does that make you feel?"

She used her hands to turn him around. It took all her strength, but she managed to do it. "I hold no illusions when it comes to who you are. I've known that all along. Regardless of what you do, you are still one of the most amazing men I have ever met. One of the gentlest human beings I've ever known. You also scare the shit out of me with your intensity. Those are all parts of you. I can't love one without loving them all. Do I agree with everything you do? No, but I understand the life you live. I'm not asking you to change. I know what I'm getting into."

For the first time since he had come home, he opened his arms for her and held her tightly to him, fisting her hair in his hand. "I'm just letting you know, I'm never letting you go. No one in this world has ever understood me more than you do, and I'm not willing to give that up."

"Good," she smiled at him as she pulled away slightly from his embrace. "Neither am I. We answer to no one about our relationship. And if you scared me physically, Tyler, you know I wouldn't be here. I know that you're dangerous, but I also know that you have boundaries. I know what those are just like you do. If I ever feel that you're getting out of control, I'll let you know."

He nodded and pulled her back into his arms. For the first time he really felt no remorse for taking someone's life, and that *did* scare him. The only consolation he had was that he knew it was for her, and for her he would do anything.

Chapter Thirty-Eight

The next morning, a soft knock sounded on the door of the dorm room. Meredith hadn't slept well the night before as she watched over Tyler. She knew that he had been very conflicted last night and she hated that. Getting up quickly, she padded over to the door and opened it softly.

"Hey," she greeted Liam. "He's still asleep."

"Just have him come up to the house whenever he gets up. Some major shit went down last night after he left."

She took a good look at the man standing in front of her. Her keen eyes noticed that he now wore the president patch. "Congrats Pres," she grinned at him.

"Thanks. I'm sorry about what William did to you, and I'm glad that we got it taken care of."

"I don't hold it against you at all. I'll let him know when he wakes up that you wanna talk to him."

She closed the door and quickly went back over to the bed, crawling in beside him and cozying up to the warmth of his body. He slept deeply, much deeper than she had ever seen him sleep before. It was almost as if this sleep healed him.

"You're not a bad person," she whispered, running her hand up and down his stomach as she listened to the beating of his heart.

"I'm a cold blooded killer," he argued, his voice rough with sleep.

This confused her. This couldn't have been the only man he had ever killed. The way he was reacting worried her.

"No you're not."

"Yes I am. I've killed before for my club, don't get me wrong. I *always* had sympathy for those men. I said a prayer for them after they died because I did feel bad. I had to do what I had to do with every one of them. With all of those it was either kill or be killed. Last night? I did it and enjoyed it."

She grabbed his face in her hands and forced him to look at her. "Because this was personal. If I had been there, Tyler, I would have done the same exact thing. You didn't do anything wrong. I don't think of you any different. I swear."

He nodded, pulling her to his body and holding her close. "That would kill me if you thought of me differently. You know I would never hurt you."

"I do," she nodded. "Liam was here earlier, he wants you to come see him. Apparently it has something to do with what they decided about William."

He sat up, running his hands over his eyes and sighed. This was definitely not something he wanted to deal with today. "Okay, I'll go see him and see what's up. Was he wearing a new patch?"

"Yeah, he had a President patch on. So I guess William got voted out."

"Or killed," he mumbled.

She ignored those words and went about finding his clothes for him. "Do you want me to come with you?"

"Nah, I gotta do this myself. My new Pres has requested my presence."

"Are you excited about Liam taking that role?" she asked as she watched him dress.

He shrugged. "It's something that's needed to happen for a while now. William was getting sloppy and complacent. We need new ideas. I think this might light a fire under everyone's asses."

Leaning down, he kissed her cheek. "I'll be back."

Tyler was not looking forward to this. Having not known what went down after he left was a huge disadvantage. Did Liam hurt William? Had he had to kill him? Was William allowed to even be a part of the club anymore? So many thoughts swirled in Tyler's head as he made his way into his new president's house.

"Hey," he called, seeing Drew sitting at the kitchen table.

"Hey, Dad's in the shower, he should be down in a few."

"What are you doing?" Tyler asked, having a seat next to the younger boy.

Drew had a magazine and a pad of paper in front of him. "Comparing protein powders. Mom said she wouldn't spend a 'gazillion' dollars," he used his fingers to make quotation marks, "on stuff I might not like or might not need. The compromise is that I do my research and she'll get me two of them. If I make bad decisions then I'm just shit out of luck."

"Language," Liam warned, coming into the kitchen, rubbing a towel through his hair.

"I know, I know."

"You wanna go have a smoke?" Liam asked Tyler as he motioned for the door.

That was the universal code for they needed to be alone and talk business. "Sure, good luck with your research. If you want any help with that protein powder, I'll stick around after I talk with your dad. I'll show you what I used to help build me up. They may not have the same brand since I'm older, but we'll try to find the correct percentage of vitamins you need."

"Would you really help me with that?" Drew asked, surprise showing on his face.

"Dude, we're buds. It's totally not an issue."

Tyler and Liam walked out of the house and had a seat on the front porch. "My son is hero worshiping you, and I'm not sure if I like it."

Tyler laughed. "Go ahead, be jealous."

They sat there blowing smoke for a few moments before Liam spoke. "We turned William over to Rooster." Funny how learning that he wasn't really his dad was okay.

"No. Shit?" Tyler said the statement in two words, slowly as he tried to absorb the words that had been spoken.

"Yeah, needless to say, he's doing some hard time for the shit that was on that cell phone."

"And this isn't going to blow back on the club."

Liam's eyes hardened. "If William wants to die, then he can try to cause problems."

That scared Tyler. The look in his friend's eyes. "I don't want this to make you into someone that you're not, Liam."

Tears pooled in Liam's eyes, and he didn't even bother to brush them away. This was his best friend. Only with Denise could he be more honest. "That man is *not* anything to me. He makes me sick. If we can't trust our leader, then who can we trust? I don't recognize him as any kind of family anymore. Now that I have my own, I can see that he never treated me or Roni the way he should have. You should never choose money and power over your family. That won't be happening in this club again."

"So what do you think we should do?"

"We're gonna have a meeting. We're gonna discuss as a group what we want to do. I think we all like the protection runs and its good money. We keep our hands pretty clean and make enough for everyone to live pretty fucking comfortably. We keep the shop and continue to fix cars, but I'm through with the drugs. That's not a chance I'm willing to take anymore, especially not with the baby coming. Wanda has contacted me too, she wants us to provide protection at the strip club when the girls leave at night. Apparently a few of them have been harassed."

"So we can still be hard-asses," Tyler grinned.

"We're all always going to have a part of ourselves that aren't fit for the rest of society, but there is no reason we can't live amongst them."

Tyler could get behind that. It felt like they were coming just a little bit full circle. Many of them were becoming family men, and while they still had a part of their personalities that couldn't be tamed, there was a part that needed to be. This was a good compromise, and he knew that Liam was the man to take them into this new phase of their club.

"You know I'm behind you completely without question."

"Good, because I need a kick-ass VP to help watch my back."

Vice President had never been something that Tyler aspired to be. He had never even thought about it. But if this is what Liam wanted, if this is what he needed, then he would gladly watch the back of his friend, his brother.

"Nobody's gonna hurt you on my watch. That I can promise."

They clasped hands, sealing their bond.

"Now before we start leaking like fucking women, let's get back inside. I think you have some more hero worshiping to attend to with my son."

"Yeah, yeah. Fuck you too, man."

Laughing they went back inside, each of them looking forward to what this change would bring. For the first time actually looking ahead to a future they could both get behind, not worried they were heading in the wrong direction. Moving forward and not backward.

Chapter Thirty-Nine

The events of the last few days had been hard on everyone. Liam and Roni had gone to speak with their mother, explaining what had gone on with William. They had come back both red-faced and subdued. A few of the older members had decided to leave the club. What remained was a young group of men who were ready to take on a new world. Ready to make a new destiny for themselves.

Tyler sat on the couch of Meredith's counselor's office, his hands between his knees. "What do you want me to say?"

"What do you want to say?" Dr. Jones asked.

He turned his head to face Meredith. "I'm not sure that I like when she answers a question with a question."

She grinned. "Sucks when someone does that to ya, huh? Remember that for when we have our own conversations."

Slinging his arm over the back of the couch, he playfully pinched her shoulder.

"Seriously, Tyler. How do you feel?"

He opened his mouth a few times to speak, but found there were no words. "I don't know. I've done many things in my life that I'm not proud of. But this felt different. This scared me."

"Why?"

"Because it felt so cold-blooded. I've never had anyone in my life who made me want to protect them the way she does."

Meredith couldn't help but beam as those words came out of his mouth. There was something so gratifying about hearing him say that. No one in her life had ever wanted to protect her.

"That's scary, huh?"

"Fucking terrifying."

Doctor Jones leaned forward, putting her hand on Tyler's knee. "That's what happens when you love somebody. Now, I'm not gonna lie to you. Most people don't put a gun to someone's head and pull the trigger to show that love, but you aren't most people."

That was the understatement of the year.

"It just feels so overwhelming," he admitted.

"Again, that's what love is. It's an overwhelming emotion that can drive some people insane, but you have to know that emotion is shared with you."

"It is," Meredith agreed. "I love you too. I know that's something you aren't used to."

"No, I'm not."

He had spent the first part of their session describing his lonely childhood and teenage years. The fact that he hadn't ever had a family to claim him. His only family for so long had been his club.

"You are loveable, Ty," Meredith whispered, leaning over to kiss his cheek.

That sweet, simple gesture opened up a floodgate of emotions in him, and she was surprised when he turned his face into her neck and she felt wetness there. He held onto her as his body shook.

Shocked, she shared a look with Doctor Jones, who looked shocked as well. Neither one of them had expected this out of Tyler.

Long minutes later, his grip on her loosened and he pulled away from her. His eyes and nose were red, his face a bit pale.

"Do you feel better?" Meredith asked, brushing his hair back from his forehead.

He inhaled and exhaled heavily. "Yeah, yeah I do."

"Sometimes all the therapy in the world doesn't help as much as a good cry," Doc Jones smiled, showing him there was no reason to be embarrassed.

"I think you might be right," he mopped up his face with his hands and shakily took another breath. "This is going to take me some getting used to, and I think I'd like to see you again, but I feel better."

"You can gladly come whenever you need to."

Meredith mumbled. "I think maybe the whole club needs to come after the stress and drama they've had the past few days."

Tyler laughed loudly. "Yeah, can we get a damn group rate?"

"I don't wanna go back," she whispered as the two of them hopped on his bike.

"Me neither. It feels like it will be stressful if we do go back," he agreed.

The dawning of December had brought with it cold temperatures. He had an idea, but there was no way they could take his bike.

"Do you trust me?" he asked.

She rolled her eyes. "After all of the things we've been through the past couple of months, you're gonna ask me if I trust you?"

"You have a point there."

Without another word, he started up the bike and drove them to the clubhouse. Once there, he parked and got off, helping her like he normally did. "Go pack a bag for both of us. Enough for a couple of days. Make sure you grab us some warm clothing. It'll be just a little bit colder where we're going. I'm gonna take my truck up the shop and make sure it's ready for a road trip. I'll be back in two hours at the most."

He didn't even wait for her to ask questions. He was gone before she could open her mouth. This man never ceased to surprise her.

A few hours later he came back with the truck properly maintenanced. "You ready?" he asked her, throwing the bags she'd packed into the back of the quad cab.

"Yeah, but I'd really like to know where we're going."

"It's a surprise," he grinned.

This must be a big surprise because she had it on authority from Denise that he'd called Liam and requested to go silent for almost a week. As new VP, she knew that was serious.

"Okay, but I'm gonna figure it out sooner or later," she taunted.

He didn't say anything else as he helped her into the truck and then took his spot behind the steering wheel. They had obviously never done a road trip together and he was surprised when thirty miles from Bowling Green, she conked out in the passenger seat. He was excited about the impending vacation. After the stress of the past few months, he was looking forward to spending some time away from the club, alone with Meredith. That would be the best medicine of all.

Turning the radio up just a bit, he took the interstate south to Nashville and then took a turn east, heading towards Gatlinburg. Hopefully, when she awoke she would be just as excited as he was.

Chapter Forty

Five hours later, they entered the city of Gatlinburg. It was bordering on late night, but he knew exactly where they were going. He had called a friend a few hours before to make sure that the cabin he wanted was available. Snow had started falling the closer he got to the cabin, but that was why he had made sure the truck was properly maintained. A few miles ago, he'd stopped and put the snow chains on his tires. Meredith had yet to wake up. He reasoned that she probably needed this getaway even more than he did.

He parked at the cabin and was glad to see the stream of smoke coming out. His friend had obviously made sure there was heat, and hopefully there would be food because after driving all the way through, he was starving. Grabbing their bags, he took them inside before going back out to get her.

"Hey," he nudged her awake carefully.

She snuggled deeply in his arms as he unbuckled her and carried her out of the truck. "Where are we?"

"Gatlinburg."

She came awake quickly. "I slept the entire way?"

He chuckled. "You must have needed it."

Rubbing her eyes, she took a glance around as he carried her into the cabin. "It's a winter wonderland out here." The pleasure was apparent in her voice.

"Sure is. I ordered the snow just for you baby."

Her small hand smacked his chest lightly. "Sure ya did."

He got the two of them into the cabin and set her down on her own feet. "I can't believe I slept all that way. I didn't even get to see the amazing views. Although," she checked her watch, "with it being almost midnight, I'm sure you can't really see them."

"We can go see them in the morning," he promised.

She turned around in a circle, admiring the cabin. "How did you get us this place on such short notice?"

It wasn't grand like a lot of them in this area were. A bathroom and bedroom were the only rooms visible off this living area that boasted a kitchen. She wondered if there was a porch with a hot tub. That seemed popular with Gatlinburg cabins.

"This is a buddy of mine's cabin. I called him and asked if he was using it, he wasn't. So here we are. Do you want to look around? It's not big."

She shook her head in a no gesture. "I just have a question."

"And I might have an answer."

She poked his arm. "Smartass. Is there a hot tub?"

"Sure is, on the back deck. We'll check that out sometime while we're here."

"Exactly how long are we here for?"

"Up to a week if you want to be."

This was more than she could have ever asked for. This was exactly what she had needed. "I'm so happy," she hugged him tightly. "We both needed this."

"That we did. I'm gonna go take a shower, would you mind making some food? I'm fucking starving. I didn't want to stop just in case the weather got worse."

"Sure," she walked to the kitchen as he walked to the bathroom.

Once there, she took stock of what they had. Someone had been kind enough to stock the pantry and fridge for them. Looking in the freezer, she saw hamburger patties. Tyler was hungry, and she couldn't believe he hadn't heard her stomach growl. Taking the patties out, she looked in the fridge and found cheese and bacon. A bacon cheeseburger sounded like the way to go. Chips sat on the counter as well as hamburger buns. She took that as a sign.

Walking out of the bathroom, Tyler ran a towel through his hair. He only had on a pair of boxer briefs, and she tried to hold back the moan, looking at his body. He really was a work of art.

"Food's almost done," she told him.

"It smells amazing. I'm not sure what it is, but I'm so hungry right now, I think I could eat shoe leather and it would taste amazing."

"Bacon cheeseburgers and chips."

He walked over to where she stood in front of the stove and slipped his arms around her waist, holding her body to his. "I love you," he whispered. He wasn't sure why he felt the need to tell her, he just knew that trying to hold it back would have required more strength than he had. He wanted to use this trip to solidify their relationship.

That had come out of nowhere. She knew it wasn't easy for him to express his emotions in words or actions, so this meant more than she could tell him. Expressing this feeling between them out loud was new, but the emotions weren't.

"I love you too," she whispered back, leaning her head against his chest and inhaling deeply.

The strength she felt there was her anchor. It balanced and centered her when she felt like everything else in the world was going wrong. Never before had she had that, and she loved that the feeling was shared with him.

"I don't know what I would do if you felt differently about me because of what I did," he started.

She reached up, putting her finger on his lips. "Stop. Don't beat yourself up. We're moving on, starting right now."

He nodded, swallowing hard as she moved the burgers from the stove and set them on buns. Within minutes they sat around the kitchen table, both eating as if they hadn't seen food in months.

"It's weird," she commented. "This food tastes better than it has in months."

He knew without her saying that the reason it did was because her attacker was dead, the man responsible was behind bars, and they could finally move on with their lives. "I think you're right about that."

They shared the meal making small talk, laughing and smiling at one another. As the food settled, Tyler yawned loudly. "I guess I'm a lot more tired than I thought," he apologized.

She yawned right along with him. Now that she could breath, she realized just how tired she was. "C'mon, let's go to bed."

He grabbed her hand, allowing her to lead him to the bed that beckoned them both. They lay down, wrapped in each other's arms, sleeping better than they had in months.

Chapter Forty-One

He was having *the* absolute best dream ever. His hands were tangled in Meredith's hair as she kneeled between his thighs, her lips wrapped around the erection that stood up from his body. He was directing her with gentle pressure from his hands as he slowly thrust his hips towards the warmth of her mouth.

Her nails scored his thighs and the slight pinch of pain brought him to reality. Quickly, he realized this wasn't a dream. This was real life. The morning sunshine streamed through the curtains, bathing her in sunlight. It looked as if she had a halo surrounding her, giving her an ethereal look.

"Damn, baby," he groaned, leaning his head back against the pillows. "Can you take it deeper?"

She opened her mouth wider, relaxing the muscles of her throat, allowing him to slip further in. Pulling him back out, she swirled her tongue around the head and couldn't help but grin as the breath hissed from between his clenched teeth.

Tyler tried to figure out how long she had been doing this because he was ready to blow. He hoped it had been enough time to make this respectable, but the visual of her between his knees looking up at him with his cock in her mouth was enough to send him over the edge. His fingers tangled deeper into her hair, pulling tighter. His hips pumped faster, his breaths becoming more and more shallow.

She went after him with everything she had, using her hand to stroke the hardness that she couldn't get into her mouth. He wrapped his big hand around hers, showing her the rhythm he needed.

"That's it," he groaned. "Back up, Meredith," he wrenched from between his lips.

When she didn't, he tried his best to hold back, but she was hitting all of his zones. He fired on all cylinders as he emptied himself down her throat, shouting hoarsely as his body kept shallowly thrusting into the warmth that surrounded him.

As soon as she pulled away, he was on her, pushing her back against the sheets. "Tyler," she whined as he lightly ran his fingers along the core of her body.

"Jesus Christ," he moaned, feeling the wetness that gathered there.

"What can I say? Giving you pleasure gives me pleasure," she smiled like the cat that ate the canary.

He quieted her as he coated his fingers with the wetness and then shoved them into her body. She thrust against him, holding his neck as she threw hers back. His lips trailed down the column of her throat, moving down to encase her nipple. As his tongue swirled the hard bead there, she arched into him, giving herself completely up to the emotions he created there.

Using his thumb, he strummed the hard nub at the top of her womanhood, eliciting a growl from deep within her throat. "Feel good?" he asked her, his voice dark.

"Uh huh."

He stayed after her, moving with her as her body moved. Using his tongue, his hands, nipping with his teeth as she thrashed against him. Her hands tangled in his hair, pulling his mouth tighter against her nipple, and she started mumbling 'oh God' as he began thrusting his fingers in rhythm with the undulations of her body. Her thighs tightened around his hand before she gave a great heave and she screamed loudly.

"There ya go," he encouraged her.

These feelings were different than anything she had ever felt either. This seemed to be another area that she was finally able to let go in. It had never been this good, never.

"Tyler," she moaned, pushing her head back against the pillow, letting her body come to rest.

"Glad I could return the favor," he grinned.

The two of them lay in each other's arms. His arms around her, her hand stroking his hair. They lay in silence for what felt like hours, but she knew it was only minutes. Glancing over at the clock, she realized it was past ten am. She really wanted to get out and do some exploring with him.

"Let's go do something," she told him, hooking her leg around his and trying to sit up.

"Do you want to?"

She nodded. "I've never been on vacation with a boyfriend before. This is a first for me."

"First for me too," he admitted to her. "Let's get dressed."

An hour later, the two of them had made their way into downtown Gatlinburg and had parked. Tyler's friend had thankfully had the presence of mind to provide them with heavy jackets. They were very appreciative as they made their way up and down the main thoroughfare.

Here it was different, since Tyler was alone, he didn't wear his cut. They walked along just like two people in love, on vacation. His large hand held hers protectively as they made their way in and out of the crowds of people. They didn't really have any plans, but they stopped at different locations and took pictures of each other with their phones. On a couple of occasions, she had kindly asked strangers to take pictures of them together. This felt blessedly normal after the months of unusual they'd both had.

"You want to go to the aquarium?" he asked as they came upon one of the tourist attractions this town was known for.

"Sure," she shrugged.

They walked up to the ticket booth, and he paid their way. Both enjoyed the exhibits and continued taking pictures with one another. As they were about to leave, a young couple with a toddler and a baby struggled to get out of the door. Tyler walked ahead and held it open for them, smiling as they thanked him. She watched, her mind going to a place she hadn't been sure it could ever go.

"Do you think that'll be us one day?" she asked quietly, holding his hand in her tight grip.

He shrugged. "That will be us if you want it to be us. I'll be with you regardless of what happens here on out, but it's up to you if we have all of that. Marriage doesn't mean kids and kids don't mean marriage. A relationship is what the two people in it make of it. We'll be whatever you want."

She loved the fact that he could take a simple question like that and turn it into something that made her think. What did she really want from him? From their relationship? Was it heading toward the altar? Was it going to be a life partnership? Did she want the kid experience with him? Everything seemed to have taken on new meaning to her in the past few days and she knew without a doubt that she had some thinking to do.

"Let's go in here," he pointed to a jeweler's shop.

Her mind heavy, she followed him, half looking at all the things that were on display.

"This is really cool," he commented, pulling her to stand next to him.

It appeared to be two necklaces. They fit together to make up a heart.

The salesperson came over, smiling at them. "I see you found our sweethearts necklace. It's kind of like one of those best friends necklaces but it's for couples in a romantic relationship. You know, it gives each one a piece of the other's heart. It's one of our best sellers."

Tyler reached into his jeans pocket and pulled out his wallet, producing a debit card. "We'll take it."

It just seemed like it was meant to be.

Later on that evening, they drove around the surrounding area, just enjoying one another's company. They passed different shops, and as they got a little further from town, it became less crowded. They passed a church that proclaimed it was a wedding chapel. They had almost passed it when she put her hand on his arm.

"Stop here, I wanna go in."

"To a wedding chapel?" he asked, his eyebrows drawn together in question.

"Yeah I do."

He knew by the tone of her voice that they weren't just going in to take a look around. He turned into the parking lot and turned the truck off. They got out and met each other around the back of it.

"You sure?" he asked.

"If you are."

Smiling he reached over and grabbed her hand. "Let's go see what kind of trouble we can get into."

Chapter Forty-Two

Meredith walked into the chapel, Tyler not too far behind. The overhead bell rang and the clerk came out, a smile on his face.

"Somethin' I could help you two with?"

Tyler reached out for her hand and squeezed it. "We were wondering what we would need to do in order to get married today."

The clerk explained the process, that they would need the names of their parents, their driver's license, and their social security cards.

"What if I was a ward of the state, and I don't know who my biological parents are?" Tyler asked softly.

"That's fine. If you don't know, you don't know. Just fill out what you can."

They filled out the information and forked over the cash that was needed.

"Do you have rings?" he asked.

They looked at one another. This was something they had forgotten.

"We don't, but we have something that's a little more us," Meredith smiled.

Tyler looked at her, the question written on his face. "Our necklaces," she explained. "And you know we could totally play with everyone like you do with your skull cup. They won't really know if we're married or not if I don't wear a ring."

The grin that broke across his face was huge. "You are learnin' so well, baby. I don't think I've ever been more proud."

She reached up, kissing him. "Are you sure *you* want to do this? I mean it's really spur of the moment."

"I firmly believe with all my heart that there was a reason we met each other. There was a reason I came upon you the night of your attack, there's a reason that we've been put together for these huge life changes. We're meant to be together. I've always been taught never to question where life takes me. God knows way more than I do. For every hurt I've ever had, I've been provided with happiness. For every hard year I've had, I've had one that was wonderful. It's all about perspective. As long as we're together, baby, nothin' else matters."

"Okay, let's go get married," she whispered, reaching up to put her arms around his neck.

He pulled her close and kissed her nose, closing his eyes to breathe her in for just a moment. The scent of her skin even drove him wild. He nodded, a bright smile on his face. This was the family he'd wanted his whole life.

Epilogue

An unusual white Christmas had descended on Bowling Green. It was a rare occurrence and even more rare that it was also freezing cold, the highs only into the teens. Inside the clubhouse, everyone was cozy and warm.

"Tyler, you have *got to stop* following me around with the mistletoe. I have stuff to do," Meredith joked good-naturedly.

Jagger called from across the room. "It's only natural, I mean you are newlyweds, right?"

Tyler and Meredith looked at one another, a smile they had shared numerous times since coming back from Gatlinburg. She winked at him and turned to face Jagger. "I don't know? Are we?"

"Damn it. The two of you are driving me up a wall. You're never going to answer that question are you?"

This time Tyler grinned at Jagger. "I don't know? Will we?"

Jagger groaned. "Bah humbug to you both."

Denise came out of the kitchen, fanning her face with a dishtowel. "Somebody else is gonna have to go in there a while. Otherwise, I'm gonna be sick on the Christmas Turkey."

She had a seat at the table, putting her head on her forearms while Liam came to sit beside her, gently rubbing her back.

"Let me help."

The soft voice came from a couple of tables over where Lauren sat with Roni making small talk. Since William had been arrested and sentenced in a quick trial, she had done her best to make peace with her children. It was still touch and go, but she had been invited to Christmas dinner, and that was more than she'd ever had before.

"I would love it," Denise smiled weakly.

She had realized early on if she accepted Lauren then Liam did a much better job of being nice.

"Just let me know what all needs to be done.

Meredith came up beside her and put her arm around the other woman. "C'mon lady, we've got a ton of stuff left yet. I'll put you to work so hard, you'll wish you would never have shown up," she joked.

"No, I'm pretty excited that I did," she whispered so that only Meredith could hear it.

Meredith winked, knowing that it had taken a lot for her to show her face. She had been glad for it, because this club needed to heal.

"Can I help in any way, Aunt Mer?"

She turned around and saw Mandy standing, waiting for someone to give her some instruction. Too young to be a woman, too old to be a child. She and her brother had grown up a lot in the past couple of months.

"Sure can. C'mon girlfriend, I'll put you to work too."

Jagger stood in the corner, looking around at the people he had begun to call family in the last year or so. Since being patched, he had felt even more at home. These people were making lives for themselves, coming out of dark places that they had resided for years and stepping into the light. He wanted these things for himself. He wanted the family that included the wife and kids (or not wife – depending on if Tyler was ever straight with him). With any luck he would have it, sooner rather than later.

Steele and Liam came out of the kitchen, cracking up. Steele pointed at Jagger, his face red with laughter. "Hey, Meredith's asking about our most memorable moments this year. Why don't you tell her about that stripper that fell buck-ass naked into your arms at the Harley Drags?"

He groaned as everyone had a seat around the tables, the women serving up the food they had finally finished preparing.

"Jagger!" Meredith reprimanded.

"I was a gentleman, I didn't look at her tits," he explained.

"What am I going to do with you guys?" she laughed, having a seat next to Tyler.

Tyler wrapped her arm around his neck and pulled her tight against him. "That's easy," he whispered. "Just love us."

She thought about it for a moment. "As long as you keep loving me."

"Then you never have to worry. We've pulled you out of the darkness, baby, and you're never going back. That's a promise."

THE END

Acknowledgements

I want to take a moment to thank all the readers that have embraced the Heaven Hill MC. I'm amazed, humbled, and flattered. You will never know how much I appreciate the word of mouth...the sharing with friends...the people who have sent me messages. This has gone so much farther than I ever expected and I have YOU ALL to thank for that!!

Michael: Thank you for always supporting me and always believing in me – even when I don't. I love you!

Allison Jewell: CONGRATS on the success of your books! I couldn't be prouder to call you my friend and my sounding board!

April: We have amazing adventures together and I hope this brings us so many more that we never could before!

My Family: I couldn't ask for better people to support me. Thank you so much for the unwavering support!

My Work Family: Thank you for being so excited for me!!

Lindsay Hopper: Thank you for sticking with me and making my stories so much better. I hope we both get where we want to be – and sooner than we think!

Kari Ayasha: I am so lucky to have found you! You do amazing work and deserve everything that's coming your way!

I know I forgot some of you, but don't think that I don't appreciate everything you do...this takes a village and I'm so lucky to have my own!

—Laramie

About the Author

Laramie Briscoe has loved romance novels since her grandmother gave her Dorothy Garlock's Tenderness as a teenager. It sparked a love of reading and writing that's manifested into this series of novels.

An avid TV and movie enthusiast, a nail polish hoarder, an obsessive book reader, and a lover of all things that sparkle and glitter. She lives in South Central Kentucky with her husband and her cat. She is currently editing the third story in the Heaven Hill series – due out late fall 2013.

She loves to hear from her readers! You can find her at:

Twitter: http://www.twitter.com/LaramieBrisceo
Facebook: http://www.facebook.com/AuthorLaramieBriscoe
Instagram: http://www.instagram.com/Laramie_Briscoe
Pinterest: http://www.pinterest.com/laramiebriscoe
Email: Laramie.briscoe@gmail.com

Coming Soon

Losing Control

Book #3 of the Heaven Hill Series

Chapter One

"Has anyone ever told you that you should be a male model instead of a biker?"

Jagger Stone froze. The husky sound of that voice had haunted him for months. Since the Harley Drags in October to be exact. It was a hell of a story really, the way the two of them had officially met. After months of watching her at *Wet Wanda's,* she'd been on the back of a truck that had been outfitted with a stripper pole. He'd caught her when she'd lost her footing and taken a tumble. She had been a lot drunk and a little naked. Since that day, he hadn't been able to get her out of his head.

"Anybody ever tell you it's not good to sneak up on a biker?"

That same voice gave a low laugh that went straight to his groin. There was something about this woman that made his palms sweat and his heart kick up a beat. Never in his life had anyone affected him this way.

"'Sneak up on a biker' is a relative term. You didn't even have your back all the way to the door. I'm sure you knew I was here."

She was right, but it wasn't because he didn't have his back to the door. Since that day she'd fallen into his arms, he'd been hyperaware of her. No matter where he was, if Bianca Hawks walked into the room, he knew it. Every part of his body knew it. She was sure to be an itch he wouldn't be able to scratch.

Ignoring her comment, he put a cigarette in his mouth and fired up his lighter. "What is a pretty little thing like you doin' here?" He flirted. Of course he knew she worked there, that was one of the reasons he kept coming in.

Here indicated *Wet Wanda's*, a bar that some of the other brothers tended to frequent. It was a dive at best. Women were sometimes up on the bar naked, and word had it you could get hand jobs or even better if you played your cards right. The clientele was right up his alley though, they loved to drink, and they loved to get rowdy when he came out to play his brand of country music that bordered on rock n roll.

Bianca rolled her eyes at the question. He acted like this was some sort of high class establishment. "Workin'. What does it look like?"

He loved the little bite of attitude she always gave him whenever they spoke with one another. He also knew that she thought she had hidden herself well from him. So he played along. "I didn't know you work here. I come in here all the time."

"I know, I see you playing."

With any other woman that would have been an automatic home run into her panties. Especially in a place like this. With her, it didn't even look like it impressed her. There was an awkward pause while he tried to figure out how to respond.

"Obviously, you're not a fan."

"Now I didn't say that," she smiled. "I just won't fall at your feet. No matter how sexy you look on stage when you play a guitar." With that she was gone.

He couldn't help the chuckle that bubbled up from his belly. With her, he didn't ever know if he was coming or going, but he loved the verbal sparring they shared.

"You ready?"

Jagger dragged his gaze from Bianca's backside and looked up at his brother, Tyler. He'd asked the question, but was obviously ready to go as he held his helmet in his hands.

"Yeah, I guess so."

Tyler laughed. "You gonna run outta here with your tail tucked between your legs?"

"What's that supposed to mean? We conversed."

"Sure you did. When that girl comes around, no matter when or where, you act like a teenage boy with a boner for the first time. You need to man up."

Jagger shrugged. "I do alright with the ladies."

Tyler put his arm around Jagger's shoulder, much like an older brother would do. He could tell that the Native American was about to impart some wisdom. "You do alright because you don't have to try. You flash those pearly whites and give that little boy grin you got, and they usually fall at your feet. This one's gonna take some work."

Not wanting to say anything that would give his feelings away, Jagger did little more than nod and get on his bike. Before he fastened his helmet, he cast a look back at the little bar and couldn't help but notice Bianca standing in the doorway.

Their eyes met for several long seconds before she broke the spell and walked back inside. His gut churned as he watched her. Tyler was right. This one was going to take a lot more than him flashing the dimple in his right cheek. He just had to decide if it was worth it or not.

Bianca had gone back inside, but that didn't stop her from looking out of a side window until she could no longer see the tail lights of the bikes. She sighed. Jagger Stone was one hot man. He turned her inside out half the time with just a grin. It was becoming an unhealthy obsession, one that had been born at one of the most embarrassing times she could ever remember in her life.

"Did he leave?" her friend Jasmine asked as Bianca turned from the window.

"Unfortunately. Hopefully, he comes back soon."

"I'm sure he will. Maybe if you were a little bit nicer to him, he might come back a lot sooner."

Bianca couldn't help the grin that came to her face. She liked to keep him on his toes, and she usually came off as bitchy. "I don't meant to be, but I can't help it. He's too pretty for his own good."

The two of them laughed and went back to serving drinks to the local group that had gathered in the bar.

Hours later, Bianca sat behind the wheel of her late model Mustang beating it to within an inch of its life. Her hands ached as she griped the steering wheel and did her best not to bang her head into it.

"Why me?" she wailed.

The cold January air seeped into the interior of the car making her teeth chatter. She'd dressed in only enough clothes to be decent In order to get the best tips at the bar, and now she was regretting it. Tucking the jacket she kept in the backseat around her body, she popped the hood and cursed as she jumped out into the elements.

She didn't know a whole lot about cars, but what she saw when she looked under the hood caused her stomach to pitch. Oil was everywhere. She fought back the initial reaction of crying. Bianca Hawks didn't cry when the going got tough. She just sucked it up and went with the punches, doing the best she could with what she had. Before she could slam the hood down on the car, she heard the roar of bikes.

She breathed a sigh of relief as they went by. Save the group that she was comfortable with, bikers tended to creep her out. When she heard the sound of a lone one coming back around, she tensed. The man who rode the bike was covered from head to toe, and he had a bandana around his face. He came to a stop in front of her and pulled his bandana away from his face.

"Hey," Jagger grinned, causing her to jump.

"You scared the ever-loving shit out of me. But I am so glad you aren't gonna murder me, I can forgive you."

"What's wrong with it?" he asked, coming around to stand beside her in front of the car.

"Oil's everywhere, and it just died on me. I really need to do some maintenance on it, but I can't really afford it."

He fiddled around inside of it and then closed the hood. "It's not goin' anywhere tonight, darlin'. I'll call Liam tomorrow and see if we can get it into the shop. Do you need me to take you somewhere?"

She eyed her bare legs and then his bike. "I'd love a ride, but I'm really not dressed for it."

Without saying a word he stripped off his leather chaps and handed them to her and then handed her the leather jacket he wore over his body. Underneath, he had on a long sleeve thermal shirt, along with his cut.

"You're gonna be wearing a patch on your back, but this is all I got."

She knew after hanging around with this group what that meant and just how much of a gentleman he was being by doing this for her. "Thank you," she told him sincerely as she put the chaps on over her bare legs and shrugged the jacket on over her body.

"You'll have to give me directions, but I'll get ya home in one piece," he yelled over the roar of the bike.

She wrapped her arms tightly around him and hung on as they sped off into the night. As with many times in her life, this night hadn't exactly turned out the way she'd planned.

The Heaven Hill Series

Meant to Be
(First in the Heaven Hill Series)

Single mother.
Laid off factory worker.
Drug runner for the Heaven Hill Motorcycle Club.

When Denise Cunningham is served with foreclosure papers on her birthday it's the last straw in a long line of bad luck. Sitting and crying about things has never been how she solved her problems, but this time she decides to do just that. A phone call interrupts her pity party and changes the course of her life forever.

Loyal brother.
Grease monkey mechanic.
Vice President of the Heaven Hill Motorcycle Club.

William Walker Jr., known as Liam to his club, needs a new recruit that is just naïve enough and desperate enough to do what he asks without question. When Denise Cunningham lands in his lap, he decides to hire her—not because he wants to, because he has to.

Neither are comfortable in their new roles, but he needs help and she can't stand to lose anything else.

As bullets fly and a local Bowling Green, KY reporter works to bring the club down, Liam and Denise find themselves getting closer to one another. When the stakes get high and outside forces try to keep them away from each other, they have to decide if they really are meant to be.

Out of Darkness
(Second in the Heaven Hill Series)

Ex-News reporter.
Rape survivor.
Former enemy of the Heaven Hill MC.

Meredith Rager's life completely changed the night she was attacked by an unknown person. Once a vibrant force that threatened everything about Heaven Hill, she is now under their care. The only place she feels safe is inside their compound. When she decides to take back the part of her life that her rapist took away, she discovers secrets that once again could tear the club apart.

Orphan.
Formidable force of nature.
Loved member of the Heaven Hill MC.

Tyler Blackfoot came into the world a John Doe. An orphan from the moment that he took his first breath, the only thing anyone knew was his Native American heritage. For most of his life, he's been alone – except for the club that has taken him in as their own. When he rescued Meredith, a protective side of his personality came out that he never knew he had. Protecting her means everything – even when he discovers danger might be closer than either of them thought possible.

Together, the two of them are trying to make a life for themselves. Against everything they have, they're hoping to see the light that will lead them out of darkness.

Connect with Laramie on Substance B

Substance B is a new platform for independent authors to directly connect with their readers. Please visit Laramie's Substance B page (substance-b.com/LaramieBriscoe.html) where you can:

- Sign up for Laramie's newsletter
- Send a message to Laramie
- See all platforms where Laramie's books are sold
- Request autographed eBooks from Laramie

Visit Substance B today to learn more about your favorite independent authors.

Made in the USA
Charleston, SC
16 September 2013